Where Honor Lies

Kindred Spirits Mysteries

Beth Connor

WOLF GROVE MEDIA, LLC

Also by

ALSO BY BETH CONNOR:

Hollow City

Lake 40

<u>The Isdralan Chronicles:</u>

Micah and the Candles of Time

Prodigy of Flame

Bridge of Blood and Thornes

Nexus of Skye

<u>Kindred Spirit Mysteries:</u>

The Secret of Misthaven Island

Bridging the Heart

The Curse at White Pines

The Last Act

I'll Be Home For Christmas

Contents

Chapter 1

Ashlyn Alden had just kicked off her shoes and sunk into the couch, easing back and enjoying the cool kiss of the evening air drifting through the open window. Outside, the murmur of the tide blended with the distant clamor of a buoy. The night was heavy with August's sweltering heat; the kind that felt sticky on skin, and made every surface feel moist, but the salt-air helped!

Then her phone buzzed.

She frowned as she checked the time. It was ten o'clock, late enough for a casual call, early enough for a crisis. After all, in her line of work, some people only called when nobody was around, too embarrassed to admit they needed the help of a psychic medium.

Ashlyn sighed and picked up the phone. The caller ID was just a number, 716 area code. Not someone she knew; maybe just a telemarketer? The allure of being home for the rest of August had appeal. It had been a long, tough year, but she knew herself better than that. She wouldn't give up the opportunity to help someone (or some spirit, for that matter).

"This is Ashlyn Alden." She said, answering the phone.

There was a brief hesitation and then a hurried voice belonging to a woman. "Ms. Alden, I really, really hope I'm not calling too late. My name's Megan Clarke. I run the historical programming at Old Fort Niagara. We have a problem."

Ashlyn sat up. A problem was an understatement or a massive overstatement; there did not seem to be a middle ground. There was nothing she could do except listen. "New York?"

"Yes, you've done ghost investigations before, right?" Megan asked, not waiting for an answer, displaying a sense of urgency in her voice. "I know you have worked with some groups that have done ghost tours here. That's why I called. We need help, and we need it quickly!"

Ashlyn pinched the bridge of her nose, willing herself to wake up. Niagara was at least a 5-hour drive. "What's happening?"

Megan took a breath before starting. "We do a lot of historical re-enactments in the summer. It's a big draw for tourists. Most of the people who participate are volunteers. History aficionados, actors looking to pad their resumes, and an occasional guy who really just loves running around in period clothing. All kinds."

"Can I interrupt you for a second?" Ashlyn asked. "You are a little further out than I usually work. Before you tell me anything too deep, do you want me to recommend someone who works closer?"

"I heard you were the best," Megan said, then she hesitated. "Please?"

Ashlyn sighed. She was a sucker for a sad voice, and Megan sounded just desperate enough to be someone watching their plans crumble. Which, based on how this conversation was already going, she probably was. It looked like it was going to be Old Fort Niagara.

"Okay," Ashlyn said. "Tell me what's happening. I'll text you my intake information when I get off the call."

"Thank you, thank you, thank you," Megan said, practically squealing. "So, every year, we do Living History. With events, actors, crowds, cannon fire, the whole bit. This time... something is not right. We have had strange accidents. Props shifting on their own, misfires, things breaking that shouldn't have at all. The last two nights, people have seen a figure on the ramparts."

"You have had ghost sightings before," Ashlyn pointed out. "Old Fort Niagara is known for these."

"Yes, but they have never been threatening," Megan said, her voice reflecting her growing frustration. "This is not something simple like an 'ooh, the tour guide heard a whisper in the tunnels.' People are quitting. If this continues, we will have to cancel the August Living History Weekend."

Now that is a problem. Ghosts... sure. Ghosts that are messing with tourism? Well, that is a tragedy.

"Maybe that is for the best?" Ashlyn replied. "I mean, fewer tourists, less overpriced kettle corn purchased, fewer sticky hands getting wiped off on your uniform when they come up to ask questions to tell you how cool you are. I mean, it sounds like a win."

"Not that easy," Megan said, becoming more frustrated talking about it. "We are a nonprofit historical society. I believe in history; however, I also believe in paying my staff."

Ashlyn sighed. Well, that was fair enough. She could respect that.

"Right," she said. "When do you need me?"

Megan exhaled with relief. "Yesterday."

Ashlyn sighed, rubbing her hand over her face. "I will be there tomorrow."

"Thanks, Ms. Alden," Megan breathed into the phone. "I will have a guest room set up for you in the staff quarters, and please, be careful."

Then the line went dead. Ashlyn exhaled and stared at her phone for a long time before forcing herself off the couch.

A headless ghost. She'd heard the stories before, but if it was coming now, amid this major re-enactment? Something had changed; it was her job to figure out what.

Ashlyn packed on autopilot, her hands moving without engaging her brain. A pair of jeans, Birkenstocks, her favorite flowy overshirt. She added a couple of breathable tops and tucked in a travel-size bottle of lavender oil, just in case the staff quarters had the unmistakable smell of mildew and regret.

She stepped over to the shelf next to the window and grabbed a small cloth pouch. Inside was a clear quartz next to an antique brass pendulum and a folded photo of her grandmother, the woman who had first taught her to listen with more than her ears. Ashlyn pressed her fingers to the photo for a second before putting the pouch into a side pocket.

After hesitating for a moment, she reached for her phone again. There was still one unread message at the top of the screen: "Let me know when you are home safe. Or when you are not."

From Rhys. A little cryptic, he always meant more than he said.

They had met by coincidence in New Hampshire, both drawn to a similar quiet town by different hauntings. He was working with a local team. Ashlyn was working on something more specific, but they crossed paths once at a diner, while drinking burnt coffee and exchanging far too many questions no one else would ask.

He was British, calm in a way Ashlyn was not, with a dry wit and low-key sadness that he never explained, and he could hear the dead, like she could. Or maybe not exactly like she could, but close enough. There was something there. A pull they never named.

Ashlyn hovered over the keyboard and typed, "Going to Niagara. Haunted soldier this time."

Then, locked the phone and put it in her purse.

The suitcase was almost full when she paused at her desk. A manila folder was sitting near the edge, still unopened from when she returned from Massachusetts last month. That case had been... difficult. Not because of the spirit - he was kind; he just further confused what was going on. No, the difficulty was the family. All denial and desperation, with intentions of cleaning things up. She had not been able to provide them with the closure they had wished for. Some hauntings were not ready to have a resolution, and some people were not ready to give their belief a chance. She shook the memories away and zipped the suitcase. There would still be time to brood on the drive.

With one last look around her apartment, Ashlyn turned out the lights. Outside, the wind mixed the faint smell of brine and honeysuckle, and the night was charged with restless energy. She could feel it tingling, that strange, heavy stillness, like someone was waiting. She just hoped it would have the decency to wait until she got there.

Ashlyn hit the road before dawn, the sky still ink-black through her windshield. She savored a travel mug of gas station coffee and tried not to think about how little sleep she'd had. The road went on in long stretches of emptiness. Headlights carved tunnels through the lingering night. The radio cycled between static until it landed, almost accidentally, on a low-frequency folk station playing something that sounded like it had been recorded on a porch a hundred years ago. The strings warbled, and a woman's voice sang about lost sailors and weeping willows. It felt weirdly fitting, so Ashlyn let it go.

The miles continued, and the scenery changed. Strip malls gave way to farmland. Cornfields bowed in the wind, and the air got heavier with each mile north. Somewhere past Rochester, the mist gathered. It crept low over the fields like something alive, curling around fence posts and drifting over the blacktop. Ashlyn rolled the window down. The morning was cool and still in a way that felt intentional. These sensations had been coming more and more bringing an overwhelming pressure behind her eyes and an odd thrum that pulsed at the edge of consciousness. Some cases heightened her awareness of her surroundings; some dulled it. This one felt like it had teeth.

She thought of the tale. The headless French soldier, Henri Le Clerc, if she recalled correctly. It was a romantic tragedy, the guides would say. He was murdered over a Seneca woman, and now he was condemned to roam the old fort, wandering for justice. Or revenge. It depended on whom you asked.

Some versions characterized him as a noble spirit, a protector of women. Others, perhaps less charitably, have suggested he had become territorial in death, more shadow than man. Ashlyn had heard it all, half-remembered tales from tourists, whispered suggestions on ghost hunter websites, and in the most extreme example of paranormal skepticism, first-hand accounts from other intuitives that there was something extra to leave Niagara spooked and pledging to never return.

She had little belief in ghost stories written by committee. The stories that get passed around, or get stitched together to reflect the good, the bad and the ugly by each account from the tour, or posts off multiple ghost hunters, where sometimes what counts is not the metaphysics of the experience, as much as the stories have come together by mere repetition rather than reality. Despite this, something was amiss in Niagara. A something that raised the hackles of an experienced reenactment team and made a practical historical director, like Megan Clarke, pick up the phone and call a psychic. This is not something people like Megan do on a whim.

Maybe it was renovations, fresh paint on old scars. Or a careless interpretation of history that was a little too close to the bone. Or perhaps, as was so often the case, something had just been buried too long, too deep for the historical record to carry. Ghosts don't stay down without a reason. They are symptoms, not causes, and echoes of something unresolved. When they reach out, they are not always angry. Most of the time, they just wanted to be acknowledged.

Mist thickened ahead of her as she approached the lake. The GPS led her off the main highway to one of only a few no-speed-limit roads, winding up to a narrow route surrounded by trees, dark, quiet, and reverent.

Just ahead, at the edge of the forest, was a figure. It didn't scare her. He was just... there. Waiting.

Ashlyn took her foot off the gas.

The man was dressed in a long blue coat with brass buttons, breeches, and a tricorne hat. Colonial clothing. No question. He stood ramrod straight, arms at his sides, head tilted toward the road, as if he was acknowledging her.

Ashlyn blinked. He disappeared.

She didn't feel scared. Ghosts often greeted her whenever she pulled up to a new place. They liked to have company who could see them. That moment of contact was never a warning; it was more of a welcome. Just a quiet "hello" from the other side.

She kept driving. The road was waiting, and so was the story. A few minutes later, she pulled through the outer gates of Old Fort Niagara. The fort rose above her, stark and weathered against the pale light of morning. Its stone walls towered over the shoreline, battered enough by centuries of wind and war. Flags waved in the distance. Inside somewhere, a spirit was waiting.

She shut off the engine. For a moment, she sat still, hands resting on the steering wheel. Then, she reached for her bag and stepped out of the car. Her boots crunched the gravel of the drive as she approached the main entrance. Whatever Henri wanted her to do, she was here now. Time to take a listen.

Ashlyn had barely made it through the staff gate before a woman strode across the gravel courtyard like a general crossing the field.

"Please tell me you have salt, sage and some kind of anti-ghost machine in that suitcase," the woman hailed, out of breath, balancing a clipboard, steaming travel mug, and a tablet (in a cracked case).

Ashlyn blinked at her. "Just the basics. And coffee. Hopefully, there is more of that."

"Thank God," the woman said. "Megan Clarke. I spoke with you last night." She shoved the clipboard under her elbow and extended a hand. "Welcome to historic Old Fort Niagara. Home of cannon fire, crumbling staircases, and … apparently, now aggressive spectral activity."

Ashlyn took her hand. Megan's grip was strong, firm, warm even in the slight chill of the morning air.

"I had no idea you were serious about the quick turn-around," Ashlyn said.

"We're on a countdown," Megan replied. She led Ashlyn across the uneven stone path. "The August Living History Weekend is our biggest event of the year, and if we don't get this worked out, I'll be fielding refund requests and dealing with angry volunteers in powdered wigs."

They passed under a stone archway. Inside, the fort opened like a storybook view: wide courtyard, tall flag poles, squat weather-worn buildings that looked like they belonged in another century.

"Nice place," Ashlyn said.

"Nice looking," Megan corrected. "Haunted as hell. C'mon, I'll show you where you're staying."

They crossed the yard toward a low building with weathered shutters and a sloping roof. Ashlyn wheeled her suitcase through the cobblestones, eyes drifting to the display of cannons and plaques marking previous battles. She could feel the past here, thick in the air, like humidity before a storm.

"There are the ramparts," said Megan, pointing with her coffee. "One of our guys took a tumble last week. Said something shoved him. Bruised a rib and almost fell on the rocks. He's not coming back."

Ashlyn looked to the place she pointed at the outer wall, the lake glimmering beyond.

"The a musket misfired two nights ago," Megan said as they passed a small stone armory. "Blank powder, double-checked. No one was hurt, but way too close for comfort."

They reached the staff quarters, and Megan opened the door. The first smell that hit her was old wood, followed by lemon cleaner, then something metallic.

"Your room's this way. It ain't luxe, but the sheets are clean, and the walls haven't bled yet. So there's that."

Ashlyn smiled. "I've stayed in worse."

"Oh, and one last thing," said Megan as she approached the door to the guest room. "We have a mannequin dressed in an entire uniform, French officer, 18th century. The mannequin keeps showing up in the wrong location. Last time it appeared in the women's restroom. In a locked stall."

Ashlyn tried to contain her expression, but raised an eyebrow.

"Yeah. So either one of our volunteers is mentally unstable, or someone very much dead has a bad sense of humour."

Ashlyn wheeled her suitcase in. The room was small but tidy, with white linens, a desk, a window just wide enough to look out onto the courtyard. The stone walls were thick, the kind that swallowed noise and kept quiet in.

"Get settled," Megan said. "I'll get the others. Zac and Naomi are in the planning room."

When Ashlyn heard the door click shut, she rested her hand on the cool stone of the window frame. She inhaled, rolled her shoulders, and headed out. Time to meet the rest of the living.

Megan led Ashlyn through a side corridor and then into what looked like a converted officer's mess that was now a planning space. The center of the room had a folding table, with maps, pieces of costume, and tangled extension cords strewn about. At the back of the table was a laptop that illuminated the face of a young man hunched over it like a monk reading from a sacred text.

"Zac, we have company." Megan declared.

The man jumped, pushed his glasses further up on his nose, and stood up a little too fast. He was wearing a faded hoodie that read Bunker Hill Battle Reenactment 2018 and jeans that had the lightest dusting of cannon soot.

"You're Ashlyn Alden," he said, nearly knocking over a coffee cup in his excitement. "Sorry. That sounded much cooler in my head. Um, I've listened to your podcast. The Haunted Histories episode with the lighthouse keeper? Terrifying."

Ashlyn smiled. "That one freaked me out, too. You must be Zac Lambert?"

"Guilty. Historian at heart, event support by title. Don't ask me how many printers this place has eaten."

"He's also our unofficial archivist, armchair theorist, and the re-enactor with the most frequent costume malfunction," Megan chimed in.

"Buttons blow up due to pressure, too," Zac muttered.

The door creaked open again, and another body stepped through, this one with the purposeful energy of someone who did not have time for nonsense.

Naomi Devaux.

Ashlyn had seen Naomi in photographs she scanned before he headed out, event posters, images of her work on a website gallery, but they didn't do her justice. Naomi's every movement was agile, the grace of someone who lives deeply in their own skin. She was wearing a dark green tunic with beadwork that shimmered in the light, and held a bundle of clothing on her arm.

"These are not regulation," she said. "This trim is synthetic, and the stitching is modern. If we are going to teach history, maybe we can stop letting it be filtered through the bargain bin polyester."

Zac gave Ashlyn a half-smile. "That's Naomi. She's.... intense."

Naomi looked up, finally noticing Ashlyn. Her stare was cool and assessing.

"You are the medium," she stated. Not a question.

"Ashlyn Alden," Ashlyn answered. "And you are Naomi Devaux."

Naomi nodded. "I've heard of you. You cleared the inn in Cape May. I read your notes."

Ashlyn tilted her head slightly. "Most people read headlines. You read my notes?"

"I care about what's left out," Naomi said, folding the waistcoat with delicate care. "Especially in relation to the past."

Her tone was not hostile, just cautious.

"Naomi's a history lover and actress who has been helping us with our Indigenous programming and keeping our history interpretations... honest," said Megan, with the air of someone wrangling two very different kinds of fire. "And she's had the misfortune of seeing our unwanted visitor."

Naomi's jaw went tight.

"I didn't see anything," she said. "Just some footsteps. Cold air. Nothing conclusive."

"You said the cold air was coming from a wall," Zac chimed in, flipping the laptop around. "And this is a still shot from the camera that Naomi set up at the ramparts."

He pressed the space bar. The screen showed a still from a security camera: empty stone, a little fog. Then, an outline. Some smoke in the shape of a man who was broad-shouldered, no hat, blurry neck.

Ashlyn leaned forward. "What time was that taken?"

"Two nights ago," Megan said. "We were firing our cannon late, and the whole platform went freezing cold. That's when Carter quit."

"And you think this is... Henri?" Ashlyn asked.

Zac nodded. "Henri Le Clerc. French officer missing in action, late 1750s. Legend has it he was murdered by another soldier over a woman. Some stories say he is protective; others, possessive. Maybe both!"

"If he's back," Megan hissed, crossing her arms again, "he's crankier than ever."

Ashlyn lingered on the screen a moment longer, the image beginning to pulse at the corner of her eye, leaving her feeling somewhat incomplete.

"He's not angry for no reason," she mumbled. "Something's happened."

Naomi locked eyes with her. "Well, let's figure it out. Before he hurts someone."

"That's my plan, but first I need to recharge after that drive," Ashlyn said.

She turned and walked out of the meeting space, beyond the activity of museum staff, the crackle of their radios, the echoing heavy military boots on worn floorboards. As she walked, the noise grew distant, consumed by thick stone walls and the deepening quiet of the private wing.

Her room lay beyond the shared public spaces. It was formerly an officer's quarters, but it had been appropriated for visiting personnel. She stepped inside, clicked the door shut behind her, and assessed the space. It had a small window that let the sunshine in, a twin bed with an end table and small dresser next to it, and there was an intense quiet. This silence was more. Something was watching.

Ashlyn leaned against the door until it settled around her. Then she began unzipping her suitcase and initiated the ritual of unpacking: toiletries, pajamas, her pouch, a small notebook. She placed the quartz on the small end table next to her bed.

As soon as she secured the quartz, the overhead light flickered, once only, as if a shuttered eye opened and closed. Ashlyn stopped and glanced up. The bulb was steady again, but there was an unusual breeze brushing the back of her neck.

She turned. The window was closed, and the frame was quite grimy with age. No ventilation. Just a breath of cold, with the faintest scent of flowers coming through. Lilacs? It wasn't that unbearable smell, like perfume or potpourri; it was a real lilac. She hadn't smelled that in months. Not since...

She shook the thought away and inspected the latch.

Outside, footsteps echoed softly up the stone path. O ne... two... three.

Ashlyn crossed to the door and put her palm on it. The wood was chill beneath her hand. Her room sat so far down the hall that there was no way someone was just 'passing' by. She glanced down at her watch. 11:11 a.m. Of course.

As she stepped out into the hallway, the bullet bulb overhead spluttered intermittently near the steep stairwell. At the far end, just before it turned, a shadow stood. Colonial clothing: a coat with breeches and boots sprinkled with cool white seaside powder. The figure never solidified. It wavered, like steam rising off asphalt. Where there would have been a head was a black nothing.

Ashlyn didn't move, and he didn't either. Then, with another flicker of the hallway light, he was gone.

She stepped back into the room and closed the door behind her.

"Well, looks like the ghost introduced himself first," she whispered, and for good measure, locked the door.

Chapter 2

Ashlyn woke to something soft pressing against her skin. For a second, she didn't move, just blinked at the ceiling, half-lulled by the muffled world outside her window and the tiredness still anchored in her bones.

Her neck ached from the odd angle of her position. She must've slept more than she intended to. It should have been just a quick nap to shake off the exhaustion from the drive, but now her head was full of fog.

The image came back to her before she could stop it. That soldier standing at the end of the hallway with the void where his head should have been. He did not speak to her, but Ashlyn knew this was Henri. Aside from the obvious fact that he was the only headless soldier associated with this place, her intuition made it very clear.

She sat up, running a hand through her hair. The light in the room was soft, early afternoon pouring through the narrow window in muted gold. Then she reached for her notebook on the bedside table, flipping to a fresh page. Her pen hovered before moving in neat, deliberate strokes.

• Flickering light–single blink

• 11:11 a.m.–timing matters?

• Cold breeze–unexplainable source

• Lilac scent–real, not synthetic

• Visual manifestation–colonial uniform, blurred edges, headless

• Felt... seen. Not hostile.

• Emotional pull is personal. Not random haunting behavior.

She paused, chewing on the inside of her cheek. Then added one more line.

• Connection to Naomi?

She set the notebook down and reached for her phone. One unread message stared back from Rhys, time-stamped just after she'd arrived.

"Met him yet?"

Ashlyn's fingers hovered for a moment, then typed back.

"He's shy. And headless."

The reply came almost instantly, as if he'd been waiting.

"Give it time. Some of them just need space…"

She smiled and wondered if he was actually talking about her. There was a warmth to his messages she wasn't ready to define, but it softened something in her, even as the comfort of it faded. Ashlyn stared at the screen for a moment longer before locking it and setting the phone facedown.

Her note taking had been a recent addition to her routine, picked up from Rhys. She had always worked on intuition and her abilities alone. Rhys shared her ability, but had developed a more analytic side to his process. With the recent addition of her podcast, this skill set had been a gift.

The room felt different now, as though the air itself was charged. She reached for the quartz still resting on the table. The stone was cool in her hand, but not inert. It thrummed ever against her skin, like the tick of a distant clock, or a heartbeat. She held it a moment longer than usual, grounding herself.

"You're not alone in here," she whispered, not afraid. Just stating a truth.

She stood and crossed to the window, cracked it, letting in the faint scent of lake air and the far-off clangs from the reenactment prep below. Once she felt more alert, she set out to begin her research.

The sunlight caught her by surprise as she stepped into the yard, its warmth blooming across her skin in a wave. For a moment, she squinted against the brightness, blinking past the stone archway that framed the fort's wide parade ground. Beyond the heavy walls, the reenactment field stretched open and bustling, costumed figures drifting across the hard-packed dirt in arranged formations. Breeches, petticoats, and weathered tricorn hats moved like parts of a living painting.

A breeze came in from the lake beyond the wall, lifting the corners of coats and snapping at the edges of flags as voices echoed across the yard. The familiar thud of boots striking the earth blended with commands and quiet laughter. Ashlyn lingered near the edge of it all, unobtrusive, letting the rhythm of the afternoon settle around her.

For a moment, it almost felt like nothing was wrong. Until her eyes found Naomi.

At the center of the formation, Naomi moved like she belonged there. She was calm, grounded, and assured. Dressed in a fitted waistcoat over linen and deerskin leggings, with her braid looped at her back, she adjusted stances with the authority of someone who didn't need to raise her voice to command respect.

The re-enactors circled around her. Some were in French uniforms, others in breechcloth and leggings. They listened as Naomi demonstrated how Haudenosaunee warriors might have observed or moved within allied drills, not in imitation, but in parallel. She described the proper gesture of greeting used when entering another camp, the way a diplomatic scout might signal peace, how an ally showed awareness without mimicking European structure. When she stepped forward, her motions carried an elegance shaped by tradition, and her open palm raised as she explained a nonverbal cue used in council diplomacy.

"Your stance reflects your intention," she told one of the younger participants. "You're not here to dominate. You're here to show respect. Your body should say that before your words do."

Not far off, Zac hovered with the posture of someone pretending not to. One hand clutched a clipboard, the other held two bottles of water like offerings he couldn't quite bring himself to deliver. He adjusted his satchel strap. Then again. Took a step forward and stopped.

"You handled that perfectly," he called, voice a touch too loud. "The way you—uh—framed the pause. That's exactly how the manuals describe it."

Naomi didn't pause, and nodded without breaking her flow, then continued explaining how Haudenosaunee delegates traditionally addressed an allied officer in ceremonial parley, standing at a slight angle, weapons visible but sheathed.

Zac lingered for another moment, then awkwardly peeled off to hand the water to a volunteer in woolen trousers who looked relieved to take one.

Ashlyn watched with a smile. Zac's interest wasn't subtle, and Naomi... Naomi hadn't shut it down. She kept her ground, not for lack of interest, but because closeness came slowly to her. Ashlyn could feel that subtle holding back; she had a way of knowing when someone was more guarded than they let on.

Naomi lifted her hand again, this time showing a stylized gesture of respect, an arm sweeping from chest to outward extension, and then the lantern flared.

It hung from a decorative iron bracket near the edge of the drill yard with an electric candle inside, unlit all day. Yet now it blazed to life without warning. The bulb flared twice before burning itself out.

A gust of cold air cut across the yard and Naomi's braid lifted behind her. She didn't move, but Ashlyn saw the way she stiffened. Ashlyn felt it, too. That pocket of wrongness.

Then the whisper:

"Onita..."

It brushed Ashlyn's ear like a word spoken through time. Ahead, Naomi faltered. A carved wooden baton slipped from her hand and hit the ground with a sharp clack. The sound cut through the yard like a spark and several heads turned.

Zac was beside her in a blink. "Are you okay?" He crouched to pick up the prop.

"I'm fine," Naomi said, voice clipped. She accepted the baton and straightened, her face smoothing into professional calm. "Just dropped it."

"You sure?" Zac asked. "Could be heat exhaustion. You've been out here a while."

"I said I'm fine." The smile she gave him was polite at best.

Zac hesitated, then stepped back.

Ashlyn kept her eyes on Naomi. Beneath the stillness, she saw the tension in her shoulders, and the subtle tilt of her head, like someone listening for something just out of reach. Something had been there. Naomi had felt it too, and this wasn't the first time. Zac's gaze lingered a moment longer before he disappeared into the building, and Naomi resumed her place as if nothing had happened.

Ashlyn ambled along the grounds with her notebook pressed against her hip. She needed a moment to let the threads of the day fall back into their pattern. The parade field behind her was full of intense energy, but as she moved toward the officers' barracks and the calmer, shaded paths that led to the old kitchens, the ambient noise and distant drill calls faded into something more internal.

The sound softened as Ashlyn slowed near a thick stretch of wall, trailing a hand along the sun-warmed stone. It was rough under her fingertips. Grounded, but the pieces still circled in her mind. Cold spot. Flickering lantern. The whisper. All targeted interaction, spiraling around Naomi.

That whisper tugged at her instincts. The spirit had given a name: Onita.

Definitely a woman's name. It hadn't sounded threatening. In fact, her impression was the opposite. There had been grief in it. Something weathered and defined. An experience, the kind that needed to be spoken aloud, as if the speaker were trying to call it back.

Ashlyn turned, directing a look back towards the parade field. Naomi stood, her silhouette stark against the orange fringe of the sun. From a distance, there was a clarity in how the disturbances assembled around her. This was not random.

Ashlyn's thoughts settled on a case she had once worked in Rhode Island. An old manor house, long ago, turned into a museum. A female spirit had hounded a guest historian for several days without letting up, following her around everywhere, even into dreams. It turned out simply because the woman wore a loose bun with a lace ribbon, just as the bride had done two centuries ago. Emotion rewrote everything.

Could this be the same? Naomi was not acting like someone who was a stranger to hauntings. If anything, she seemed put out, like someone too busy for ghost drama. A defense mechanism, perhaps? Or... history. She made a mental note to ask Naomi if she had dealt with things like this before.

Then there was Zac. Ashlyn could not get the image of his distress for Naomi off her mind. He knew more than he was letting on.

She narrowed her eyes. Was he being targeted too? She had seen it before. Spirits, who started out subtly. Flickers of anxiety, strange dreams and physical marks. Little things that escalated.

The smell of burnt coffee grounds and lemony cleaning spray hit her nose before she entered the kitchen. The staff lounge was tucked in beside the storage closets. It was a squat little room with peeling linoleum, low-buzzing fluorescent lights, and a fan in the ceiling that turned with little effort to filter the hot air. Zac was hunched over at the square table in the corner, fingers gliding across his phone's screen, with a half-drunk can of soda by his elbow. His knee bounced under the table, and from the upside-down viewing angle of his screen, Ashlyn glimpsed a familiar forum header: Aggressive Entities or Just Bad Vibes? Her mouth twitched. She was careful not to announce herself, though her boot gave her away with a soft squeak from the floor.

Zac jumped and sat up, almost spilling his drink. "Holy—sorry!" He rubbed his neck, obviously startled. "I didn't hear you."

Ashlyn held her hands up in mock surrender. "Didn't mean to sneak up on you. Although I have a little of a reputation."

He chuckled and turned the phone facedown. "You would think working at a haunted fort would make me less jumpy."

"You would think that." Ashlyn stepped toward the counter, picked a mug from the drying rack, and poured herself half a cup of coffee.

"Want some?"

"No, I'm good. I'm pretty sure I've hit my caffeine quota for the week."

She slid back into the chair across from him, folding one leg under the other as she studied him over the rim of the mug. "Long day?"

He stopped short, then nodded a small nod. "Yeah. You could say that."

Ashlyn let the silence hang, just long enough to allow for honest conversation. She didn't push. "You know," she said after a second, "for someone who's just tasked with managing tech and props, you looked pretty concerned when Naomi dropped that thing."

He blinked, taken aback, but didn't deflect. "I mean… yeah. Wouldn't you?"

"She told you she was fine," Ashlyn said, keeping her voice quiet. "But you didn't trust her."

Zac didn't answer right away. Instead, he ran both hands across his face, fingers dragging through his hair, and setting his hands in his lap.

"Something is happening," he said, voice quieter now. "Not just to her. To me."

Ashlyn nodded once. "Go on."

Zac scanned the small kitchen as though the buzzing light fixture above them was listening. He cast his eyes toward the hallway, then the window above them seemed to catch his attention, and finally, he returned his gaze to her. He leaned in closer, voice low.

"My flashlight keeps turning itself on at three a.m.," he said. "Every time. On the dot. Like the same invisible hand turns it on."

He stopped, waiting for her to laugh, but Ashlyn just listened, mulling it over and encouraging him without pressure.

"Initially, I wondered if it was a short or that I shoved it in my pack and hit the button accidentally. But then—"

He paused and licked his lips.

"My laptop restarted on its own a couple nights ago. I was asleep, but when I woke up the screen was glowing and there was a Word doc running. I don't remember opening anything, and it was absolutely not anything I had written. Just... gibberish."

"Gibberish?" Ashlyn tipped her head, already categorizing the words in her mind under Manifestation, Communication Attempts.

"Yeah, just like random letters, like someone rolled their hands across the keys. Except—" He lowered his voice lower. "In the middle, there were three words. Like the someone stopped the mashing to... type."

She stared at him. "What did it say?"

"Je vois toi." He paused. "French. I see you."

Ashlyn's grip on her mug tightened. Her face didn't change, but tension coiled up her spine.

"That might be something," she said, her voice still calming.

Zac let out a short laugh. "No. It's really not."

He fidgeted with the can, spinning with his thumb. Then he appeared to force himself to sound nonchalant and reached for the neckline of his t-shirt, tugging it aside.

Ashlyn leaned in to see. Three thin, parallel lines curved across the upper right of his chest, red and still scabbing healing.

"Did they bleed?" she asked.

"A little," he admitted. "I thought maybe I'd scratched myself in my sleep, but the angle doesn't make sense."

Ashlyn sat back, her face neutral, but her mind was racing. Flashlight activity. Digital interference, time specific manifestations, scratches. Classic escalation.

She scrutinized Zac. His knee was bouncing again under the table. The corners of his lips pulled tight as if he had been clenching his jaw too much lately and his eyes looked like he hadn't slept in days, rimmed red.

"You said this started after Naomi was first targeted?" she asked.

He nodded. "Yeah. A day later, maybe less. At first I thought it would be just stress. She's been wound up. Everybody is a little on edge." He blew out a long breath. "It just feels personal, like I am being stalked. Not in the 'it's a haunted house' kind of way, but more in the 'I don't know' kind of way, like I'm being measured or evaluated."

Ashlyn's fingers tapped the ceramic of her mug, slow and intentional, while the pieces in her mind shifted again. Maybe it was warning him off.

What if Henri was not just bound to the fort but bound to someone in it? Who was Onita? She needed to start research and collect facts before she began making conclusions.

Still, what if Henri had once loved this Onita? What if that love had never died? If Naomi carried some echo of that woman, it was possible that the presence was not malicious at all! But Zac...

Zac might look like competition.

"You are scared," she said, watching his fingers as he played with the soda tab on his drink.

He lowered his eyes. "Yeah," he said after a while. "A little."

Ashlyn grabbed her notebook, turned to a blank page and her pen scratched across the paper.

• Zac-flashlight goes off at 3 a.m.

• Laptop restart - Word doc with the phrase: Je vois toi

• Physical manifestation-three scratches across chest

• Escalation begins one day after Naomi targeted

She paused, tapped her pen against the margin. Then added another note in the bottom corner, smaller than the others.

Jealousy? Henri = protector. Henri sees Zac as a threat to Onita/Naomi?

Closing the notebook with a soft snap, Ashlyn looked up to see Zac's eyes on her.

"This isn't random," she said. "He is purposefully choosing who to engage with."

"You think it's Henri?"

"I think something's been stirred up. Henri or something else... I'll get to the bottom of it."

Zac gave a weak chuckle and rubbed the back neck, as if trying to dislodge the ball of fear stuck there. "You're really good at this."

Ashlyn smiled. "It's all in a day's work."

She stood and gestured toward the door. "Come on, let's go catch the end of practice. Maybe we will have an opportunity to talk with Naomi as well."

They stepped into the hall and down to the courtyard, where the rehearsal was wrapping up. That's when Ashlyn saw him.

The man emerged from behind the shadow of the armory like a bad idea. There was something unsettling about him, and Ashlyn was on high alert. The man was tall, broad-shouldered, with a rolled-up canvas tent bag on one arm, and a prowling gait that looked like trouble.

He looked to be in his mid-to-late thirties, with a face so unremarkable it was almost unsettling. Patchy gray stubble shadowed his chin, and his jaw was clenched too tight, like he was chewing on anger. His eyes swept the space with the cold precision of a predator surveying a room full of prey. Every movement was reactive, like he might snap without warning. Ashlyn did not know him, but she could tell everything about him on instinct. Unsafe.

The man made a beeline for Naomi, pushing through the dispersing volunteers without a second glance. People moved instinctively out of his path, like a flock scattering.

Naomi turned at the sound of her name. Her expression didn't change, but her shoulders pulled inward with a shift so subtle it would've gone unnoticed if Ashlyn hadn't been watching closely.

He stopped too close. His hands cut through the air as he spoke with quick, jabbing motions that felt more like prodding than emphasis. Ashlyn couldn't make out the words from across the yard, but the energy was charged.

Naomi stepped back leaving just enough room to carve out space that hadn't been offered. Ashlyn saw it. And she wasn't the only one.

Zac had paused beside a teetering stack of plastic chairs, half-heartedly pretending to straighten the pile. His eyes were locked on Naomi, his mouth drawn tight. He took a step forward, hesitated, then shifted his weight, one hand tightening around the back of a chair. The urge to intervene was visible, but he stayed rooted in place. Whether it was fear, uncertainty, or simply the understanding that Naomi didn't need saving, Ashlyn couldn't tell.

Ashlyn stepped up to him in a whisper, "Who's that?"

"Marcus," Zac answered without breaking his stare. "Another re-enactor that thinks he owns the place."

"He also has a thing for Naomi," Zac interrupted, as if reading her mind.

Naomi seemed unfazed. She replied with some brief words they didn't hear. Marcus's face pinched, and Naomi turned and walked away, her braid swinging low and slow across her back, unhurried but not looking back.

Marcus stood frozen, tension carved into his jaw. His eyes stayed locked on her like someone that didn't know how to let go.

A gust of wind swept through the courtyard, and one of the decorative lanterns mounted to the armory wall flared and extinguished. Marcus jumped, and his head jerked as if something had skimmed past. He spun and looked around, but there was nothing. Just the flicker of his shadow creeping toward the stone wall.

A ripple ran down Ashlyn's spine as she watched Marcus move off, humming to himself. He didn't see her, but

Naomi did. As she crossed the yard, their eyes met. Naomi gave a small nod. Ashlyn returned it.

She didn't follow.

There was too much stirring, too many emotions. Whatever had just unfolded between Naomi and Marcus was too tangled to touch. Some truths needed room to unspool.

So Ashlyn filed the encounter away, quietly recording Marcus in the same mental ledger that already held whispers in French, unexplained lights, and lilac-scented air. It was time for the facts. Research tells you what feelings can't. Ghosts weren't the only things that lingered, and not all hauntings came from the dead.

Later, back in her room, Ashlyn sat cross-legged on the narrow bed, notebook in her lap, pen tapping absently against her lip as the day rewound in her thoughts. The last of the light had quietly dissolved, and the fort had slipped into that late-hour hush.

She turned to a fresh page and wrote.

• Naomi-calm exterior, carefully tended

• Persuaded by flickering lantern, whisper "Onita?"

• Repeated indications support personal fixation

• Spirit is attracted to her. Emotionally distant. Potentially guarding.

• Onita = historical figure? Personal name?

• Zac-marked (three scratches), 3:00 a.m. flashlight, laptop disjunction

   • Phase "Je vois toi" = personal communication

   • Escalation suggests targeted action. Could be a rivalry.

   • Spirit discontent? Trying to intimidate?

   • Marcus-aggressive approach causing Naomi distress.

   • Lantern flared + extinguished around him

   • Spirit intervening? Protecting?

She circled "Onita" and scratched a light line connecting "Onita" to Naomi's name. Then drew another, thinner line from "Onita" to Zac's. A triangle.

She reached for her phone on the bedside table and typed out a quick text to Rhys.

"You ever deal with a ghost that displayed jealous behavior?"

She hadn't expected a response tonight. His hours were notoriously unpredictable. But the reply came before she'd even set the phone down.

"Yes. More than once. They don't let go."

Putting the phone down, Ashlyn moved to the window and placed her palm against the glass. Outside, the courtyard was still and the lantern, near the path to the barracks, was glowing a dull orange.

Then it blinked twice. This wasn't the weather tugging at a loose connection or the idle stammer of faulty wiring.

It had rhythm, almost like a message. Whatever lingered in the dark: ghost, grief, or something else, was no longer simply haunting. It had chosen its players. Now it was waiting to see how the story unfolded.

Chapter 3

Water lapped at the shoreline, moonlight streaking silver across the surface of the lake. A woman stood just past the reeds, barefoot, with long hair that was damp as river grass. She turned, and the red glint of a blood moon flickered in her eyes. Some distance behind her, the hollow sound of metal scraping stone echoed through the ruins of a courtyard.

Then, without warning, a figure stumbled forward. No face, only the wet sucking of mud against the boots, and a dark bundle clutched tight in his arms.

Ashlyn jolted awake, skin clammy under the sheets. The faceless man etched into her mind, stitched like a fabric of fog creeping through the windowpanes. She sat up and rubbed her eyes, letting the dream dissipate. This was definitely a sign. She slipped on a hoodie and padded to the kitchenette, grateful for the half-empty carafe of coffee that was still warm. The clink of a mug and the crinkle of the wrapped apple turnover grounded her.

With mug in hand, she returned to her room and took out her laptop. Her fingers hovered for a moment, then with a soft sigh and a sip for steadiness, she typed: Old Fort Niagara ghost stories.

The article came up first: "The Headless Haunting at Old Fort Niagara". Ashlyn clicked it, knowing the tale already. The page opened with an old sketch of a man in an 18th-century French uniform. Underneath that was the story. According to the article, the French officers would sometimes request Seneca women from a village a few miles away to come to the castle for evening events. This was not hospitality; it was political posturing. Ashlyn visualized the flickering candlelight against the stone walls and the laughter conflicting with colonial guilt. One lady present was named Onita. The article described her as quiet, sharp-eyed, and proud. As far as Ashlyn could tell, it was Henri Le Clerc, a young French officer, who first took notice of her.

The name Onita surprised Ashlyn, ash she had not known that detail before, but seeing it on the screen sent a shiver of exhilaration through her body. It confirmed that what she was following was real, not just chasing shadows. She kept reading.

Another officer named Jean-Claude de Rochefort also became fascinated by Onita. The article described how the resentment of the budding relationship between Onita and Henri grew. One evening, after drinking too much wine and not having enough sense, they got into a sword fight. Their duel was supposed to be a private show of honor and bravery. Unfortunately, something went wrong; Henri fell and hit his head, rendering him unconscious. In a drunken panic, Jean-Claude finished the job.

What happened next read like a horror novel. Perhaps out of guilt, Jean-Claude attempted to hide the murder by dragging Henri's body through the castle halls. Eventually, he hacked off his head, wrapped it in the castle tablecloth, and went to toss it into Lake Ontario. He intended to make it look like it was the handiwork of hostile combatants. The article stated he was mopping up blood off of the stone floor with shaking hands when he heard voices coming from above. Officers and their companions coming back down from the party upstairs. With no time left to finish, Jean-Claude threw the body into the castle's central well and ran off with the head.

Ashlyn blinked, her hand hovering over the trackpad. It took days for anyone to ask where Henri had gone, and he was ultimately declared a traitor and deserter. Onita never believed he had left. Instead, she distanced herself from the castle parties to mourn and conduct her own inquiries.

Months later, on a late September night with a blood moon, she returned to find answers. She walked the grassy castle grounds with another officer. There were no witnesses, but the two of them were reportedly near the well when they heard a strange scraping sound they described as steel being dragged along stone.

Ashlyn breathed quickly; she could hear the sound from her dream. Her fingers moved almost of their own accord as she bookmarked the article, highlighted passages, and copied the source. She reached for her notebook. Time to follow the clues.

It was late morning when Ashlyn finally left her room. The fog outside had cleared a little, but the fort was still damp and unusually quiet. Clutching her notebook to her chest, she crossed the courtyard towards Megan's office, her footsteps echoing off the old stone.

The moment she entered, Megan looked up. "How is the investigation going? Is there anything that you need?"

Ashlyn dropped into the chair across from her desk, already flipping through a page of scribbling. "I have been researching Henri Le Clerc. The article mentioned a duel, a missing head, and a Seneca woman named Onita - it's... more than just a legend. I think there might be truth to the story."

Megan nodded thoughtfully. "It is one of the most popular ghost stories around here. We have had many accounts of various experiences over the years. People have definitely seen Henri by the well, but nothing where he is aggressive. He appears to remain in that spot."

Ashlyn leaned forward. "Could I potentially get access?"

"The well? It's sealed, and also off-limits to the public, but sure, I will give you a key. Just watch your step. Those stones are older than anyone alive."

"I was hoping to go at nightfall," Ashlyn added.

Megan hesitated. Then shrugged her shoulders. "Fine by me. Just let someone know you're leaving. The grounds can get... weird at night."

Before Ashlyn could respond, there was a knock at the door. Zac poked his head in, looking a little sheepish. "Sorry to interrupt," he said, "but I was wondering if I could join you tonight... for the investigation, I mean."

Ashlyn looked over at Megan and then nodded. "I never do these alone, not anymore, and it's one less thing on my checklist."

Zac's smile was a little too bright, and then it seemed like he'd remembered something. "Oh yeah, that wasn't the only reason I came in. I was doing the morning equipment check, and - um - one of the muskets - it didn't have blanks."

Megan stood up so suddenly her chair skidded against the floor. "What do you mean? It didn't have blanks?"

"I mean it had a live round," Zac said. His flushed face paled. "Real powder. Real shot. I triple-checked it."

Megan's face went white. Then red. "We do not keep live ammunition on site. Ever. And that is not something that just... shows up." She breathed in through her nose. "Thank you for catching it. Bring all the firing props to my office immediately. Rehearsals have no props until I figure out what's going on."

"Yes, ma'am," Zac answered, already halfway out the door.

When it closed behind him, Megan sagged against her chair. "I'm going to have to call the police," she said. "You don't think this is something a ghost would do, do you?"

Ashlyn shook her head. "Ghosts mess with power, knock things over, trigger fear responses. They don't exchange blanks for live ammo. That's human."

Megan let out a long sigh of exasperation. "What else do you need before I make this call? I can help. But if one more thing like this happens, I swear I will cancel the entire damn event."

"I need to set time with Naomi Devaux, and someone who actually knows the history of the era," Ashlyn said, then flipped her notebook shut.

Megan tapped her pencil against her lips. "Naomi's your best shot for any info on Seneca. She's sharp and knows what's real and what's been romanticized. Believe it or not, Zac is sort of our unofficial historian. He's got access to all the site records and has a tendency to remember the details none of us do. It could be your best combo. And clearly, he's taken a shine to you. Some of the staff can be a little... stiff."

Ashlyn nodded, already envisioning the duo. "That's perfect. Naomi and Zac."

She didn't say it out loud, but she felt the corners of her mouth twitch upward. Ghost whisper by trade, match-maker by instinct.

"Alright," Megan said, standing up. "I'll text you the times and meeting spots once I get them. Until then, the grounds are all yours. Just be careful."

While Ashlyn waited for Megan to get back to her, she roamed around the outer grounds of the fort, her note-book forgotten in her satchel, arms out relaxed at her sides. She walked, eyes half-lidded, barefoot, on a section of grass extending just past the French Castle. It was a practice she didn't always explain — skin to soil, like grounding a wire. The energy moved through her in gentle pulses, as delicate as breath.

Some places felt cold, and not because of the temperature, but because they felt like a memory with the history scraped clean. Or warm, like electricity, buzzing under her skin. There was grief near the barracks and static tension by the stone wall lining the end of the old parade ground. The courtyard by the sealed well delivered vibration just under her sternum.

Ashlyn paused there, her hand resting lightly on the stone. She didn't force a connection. Instead, she listened. A flicker went by in her sight: moonlight on stone, a shadow zipped past candlelight, the echo of laughter turned sharply. A sword? She blinked, and it was gone. The draw of something lighter pulled her focus. Music.

She followed the sound, drawn by the lift of melody. After emerging from the stone archway to the outer courtyard, there was a small group of re-enactors under a white canvas tent with period instruments: two fiddles, a wooden flute, a bodhran drum. The group played a lively French-Canadian folk tune, which was once intended to lift spirits after long marches and bitter winters.

The music was playful, with flurries and foot tapping. One fiddler recognized her and nodded mid-phrase. The young woman nearby clapped and swayed to the melody. Ashlyn sat on the edge of a barrel and allowed her breath to slow.

The energy here felt different. Lived-in, not haunted. Whatever lingered at the well or the barracks was leaving this space alone. She let the music move through her body while her eyes drifted closed, the flute trilling above the steadfast heartbeat of the drum.

The laughter came first. Not the re-enactors', but softer, like a voice from the past calling across time. The warmth of the sunlight was fading from her skin, and the stillness of the stone, tinged with candlelight, folded around her. When Ashlyn opened her eyes, she had stopped watching the rehearsal.

Instead, she stood outside a banquet hall full of firelight. Men and women danced in gentle arcs to the same notes, now being played ages later. The air shimmered with pipe smoke and perfume, every breath tinged with wine.

Henri Le Clerc stood at the center, a crisp blue uniform and a smile that could only come from drink and joy. He moved effortlessly with a young woman in a white dress embellished with red beads. It had to be Onita, shining and laughing beneath a tangle of dark hair. They barely skimmed the stone floor as they turned, present only to each other.

A man stood at the edge of the space, half-hidden in the shadows behind a pillar. His eyes were narrow with envy, the line of his mouth stiff, fingers white-knuckled and clenching a glass that had not left his hand. For a moment, it felt like he was staring not at Henri, but at Ashlyn.

The flute made a shrill, aching note. Blink.

She was back on the barrel with clammy hands and shallow breath.

The music still played, but the world had reclaimed its form. The fiddler called for a break, wiping his brow and sharing a joke with the drummer. No one else appeared to feel disturbed. Ashlyn sat still and silent, the ghost of that dance still needing to breathe. She pulled out her notebook and scrawled a single line before the memory faded:

He had been watching them long before the duel.

Ashlyn was still scribbling furiously in her notebook to capture all the details of the vision before they started fading away, when she heard quiet footsteps. She looked up to find Zac standing just a few steps away, hands in his pockets, and a hopeful-but-awkward smile at the corner of his mouth.

"Megan said you needed help with historical research?" he mumbled, so as not to disturb any of the remaining musicians tuning their instruments. "She also wanted me to let you know Naomi will meet you at about three. You can use Megan's office; she'll be off site this afternoon."

Ashlyn straightened her posture, stretching out her legs as she rose from the barrel. "Right on time. I could definitely use a second set of eyes, and someone who won't roll their eyes when I ask weird questions."

Zac laughed and rubbed the back of his neck. "Good news. I'm a historian. Weird questions are kind of what I do."

He led her through the courtyard and into a side building just off to the right of the main exhibit hall. The hallway was quieter with the original stone walls, and a faint smell of old paper mixed with linseed oil hung in the air. At the end of the small hall was a locked wooden door with a small brass plaque: Research & Archive Access - Staff Only.

Zac pulled a key from the lanyard around his neck and unlocked the door. The air inside was cool and dry, kept at a temperature to help maintain the many wood and leather-bound books, archival boxes, and flat drawers. A long wooden table stretched the length of the room, scattered with acid-free folders and a few padded book cradles, and a scanner sat powered off in the corner, providing a quiet hum. It wasn't a library, but it felt much older than the building surrounding it.

"We have a fairly robust collection of French and British military records, muster rolls, personal letters, and translated officer reports," Zac started, flipping on the overhead lights. "The French ones are more challenging. Some were copied from overseas archives, but Megan has done well to keep them indexed."

Ashlyn stepped toward the shelf Zac was pointing at, running her fingers along the labeled boxes. "Would there be anything here that would cover officer incidents or duels? Something that is relevant but not formal enough to be included in the official reports?"

Zac rocked back and forth on his feet. "There might. Quartermaster reports could include some disciplinary memos. Some of the French captains liked to leave a few passive-aggressive notes in the margins." He smirked. "French bureaucracy. Gotta love it."

Ashlyn smiled, but her eyes were distant already, scanning the boxes as if they might start talking to her.

"Let's start here," she said, grabbing a folder titled Fort Niagara - French Garrison, 1758-59. "And just keep an eye out for anything unusual. Missing names. Transfers that don't add up or someone being reassigned after a fight."

Zac grabbed a second folder and sat next to her. "Henri and Jean-Claude, right?"

"Plus Onita," Ashlyn replied softly, cracking open the front folder. "She's the linchpin holding it all together."

The next hour slipped by silently, with just the sound of paper, notations, and an occasional whispered question. Zac was mechanical, cross-referencing names and dates. While on Ashlyn's part, it was much more instinctive, letting her fingers linger across the pages, eyes wandering toward the margins, half-hoping something would leap out with purpose.

"Wait here!" Zac said suddenly, jabbing a column in a brittle muster roll. "Henri Le Clerc. Lieutenant, as attached to the main garrison. Logged in from March to mid-August 1759... then nothing."

Ashlyn leaned in, nearly onto his shoulder. The handwriting was tidy enough. Only four months written of presence, a long line of check marks filled the left margin next to each month next to a record of presence, until August, where a faded dash replaced the mark.

"No note?" she asked.

Zac shook his head. "Normal protocol for someone when they get reassigned, killed, or disappear is to write it in the remarks column. This just... nothing."

"Like he disappeared," Ashlyn said, and she returned to her folder: Quartermaster supply notes that were covering the same period. Nothing more than weapon repairs, food rations, and uniform shipments. The same mundane things you would expect in a military quartermaster's notebook. Then, almost lost between two lines about boot inventory, she saw it. "Cleaned excessive blood by the entrance to the well. Weather dry, and no recent rainfall to account for pooling. Notified Capt. Rochefort. No further action taken."

Her breath caught. She traced the sentence with one finger. The date matched Henri's last check-in.

"Zac," she said, sliding the page over to him. "Look at the name. Rochefort."

He took it, eyes barely wide. "Jean-Claude de Rochefort. The captain was in charge that month. You think—"

"I think we just found the after-the-matter cleanup from the murder." She breathed. "No report of a body. Just... blood. And then nothing at all."

Zac looked white as it set in. "And if Rochefort wrote the report himself—"

"Then he was covering it." Ashlyn leaned in, excitement spilling into her bloodstream. "This isn't just a ghost story; it's a crime that has been buried."

She pulled out her phone, took a full-page photo of the entry, removed the page, and put it back in the folder. For a moment, they stared at the wall, and then neither spoke.

Then Zac said, "We're going to find his head, aren't we?"

Ashlyn didn't answer right away. She closed the folder, her mind drifting back to the well that had been sealed off and the scraping sound she had thought she had heard in her vision.

"I think," she said finally, "someone has been waiting for a long time for someone to listen to him."

She remembered her dream and the man stumbling through the dark, his arms wrapped around the bundled cloth. If the head had been thrown into Lake Ontario, they may never have found it. Maybe that wasn't the point.

Ashlyn closed the last folder and slid it into its sleeve while the clock on the wall chimed three. The energy in the room had shifted. Less discovery, more anticipation.

"I should get going," she said, stuffing her notebook into her satchel. "Naomi's waiting."

Zac nodded but stayed in his chair, drumming his fingertips lightly on the table. "I wish I could go with you," he said before adding, "but I've got inventory checks this afternoon. Megan is a ball of nerves."

Ashlyn gave him a smile. "That's alright. Meet me in my room about 10 tonight. We'll start our investigation after lights out."

His face lifted, a mix of nervous and excitement. "Yeah. Yeah, okay. I'll be there."

She paused, her hand on the doorframe. "Bring your flashlight. And maybe something you can ground yourself with. Just in case."

Zac gave her a shaky thumbs up. "Roger that, ghost boss."

Ashlyn grinned and slipped out into the hallway, her feet already leading her to Naomi, and hopefully on to the next layer, to the truth.

When she knocked on the door to the office, it was already slightly ajar, and Naomi's steady voice called from inside, "Come in."

Inside, Naomi was seated at her desk, with a mug of tea in one hand and the color-coded program schedule in front of her.

"I hope I'm not catching you at a bad time," Ashlyn said as she stepped in.

Naomi smiled. "There is never a good time during event week, but this is probably the best you will get."

Ashlyn smiled back and then sat across from her. "I wanted to catch you up on what Zac and I found in the records."

At the mention of Zac's name, Ashlyn caught Naomi's eyes lift just barely. There was something quiet, unspoken there. She filed it away.

"We reviewed the muster rolls and some supply records. Henri Le Clerc drops off the log in August 1759, and is never explained," Ashlyn said. "But there is a supply note that mentions blood being cleaned by the well, no report of an injury. Signed, Captain Jean-Claude de Rochefort."

Naomi did not interrupt, but her grip on the teacup tightened.

Ashlyn took a breath. "There is more. I've been picking up... impressions. A vision, I guess. I saw Henri and Onita dancing together at a gathering, and Jean-Claude watching them from the shadows. The air shifted, fading into something that felt like memory or echo."

Naomi observed, neither dismissing nor embracing what she was hearing. Her silence suggested deep deliberation.

"I wanted to meet with you for two reasons," Ashlyn continued. "One, your knowledge about the history and traditions of the Seneca people. Two, the ghost interaction I saw near the well yesterday."

Naomi exhaled, and her lips thinned. Ashlyn could almost see the internalizing. When she spoke, Naomi's voice was very soft.

"There was an interaction. But that's not rare. This land has layers. Not all of them are violent."

Ashlyn leaned in forward. "So, more than one layer? Can you share your thoughts about what you think is happening or what it might mean in terms of Seneca beliefs?"

Naomi sat up a little straighter. She seemed cautious in her tone. "I can tell you what I know, but I don't speak for the Seneca Nation, or the Haudenosaunee people, for that matter. Each family and community has its own teachings. What I say is based on my experience, and what my elders taught me."

"Of course I get it," Ashlyn acknowledged with a nod.

Naomi set her tea down. "Our relationship with the dead isn't like what's in movies. Spirits don't hang around to scare us. They stick around when something is unsettled, when a break in the natural cycle of return has occurred. Sometimes they stick around because we called them back. Sometimes, they are here because no one is sending them off."

Ashlyn thought about that. "So you think Onita, or even Henri, might be here because something was broken?"

"Maybe." Naomi tilted her head. "Or maybe someone wants them to be here. Grief has its own gravity."

Ashlyn let that settle in, then said, "Do you think there might be some records somewhere outside the fort? Something about Onita. Oral history, family names, stories?"

Naomi picked her mug up again and looked thoughtful. "If something is written, it would be in the fort archives. Women like Onita didn't get into colonial records unless someone documented them, and not usually kindly. Oral history? That's possible. Stories of women who dealt with soldiers or mysteriously vanished... those exist. You'd have to find the right people. It will not be in a folder."

Ashlyn nodded along, appreciative of their honesty. "Would you want to help me do that?"

Naomi paused, then gave a slow nod. "If you're willing to listen more than you ask."

"I can do that."

Naomi looked at her, searching for something, then gave just the slightest smile. "Then we'll see where it takes us."

Ashlyn hesitated for a moment and then said, "Would you consider coming with us tonight for the session? When Zac and I try to make contact?"

Naomi's face shifted to neutral. She put her tea down and folded her hands in her lap.

"I appreciate the offer," she said, her voice steady, "but I have to be honest with you. That kind of work...it's not something to take lightly. I was taught to respect the spirits, not to call them."

Ashlyn nodded, not surprised, but still curious. "So you don't believe in contacting the dead?"

"I believe the dead are already talking," Naomi said. "You don't need tools or ceremony. You just have to listen. If you feel the need to call them on land like this, you are stirring things that don't want to be stirred."

Ashlyn let the quiet settle into their conversation before gently asking, "So that's a no?"

Naomi's lips turned, but not unkindly. "That's a not tonight. I have to keep myself anchored and grounded with everything else going on, but I'll stay nearby. If something happens, or if you need help processing what you find, I'll be available."

Ashlyn smiled. The answer was what she had assumed and somehow felt more significant because of it.

"That's fair," she said. "To be honest, I think that's one of the things I like about you."

Naomi raised a brow, amused. "What thing?"

"Your center. You don't shy away, and you know who you are, and where your roots are." Ashlyn's gaze drifted down to her hands and then back up to Naomi. "I'm used to watching people get spooked when I bring up visions and voices. You don't do that. You listen to me. Even when you don't agree."

Naomi held her gaze, and something shifted between them.

"I try to stay steady," she said. "Even when the ground isn't."

Ashlyn nodded. "Well, if you change your mind, there is a spot for you at the table. But either way, I am glad you are part of this."

Naomi gave a small smile and lifted her tea in a toast.

"Just don't go calling anything you can't send back," she said.

Ashlyn grinned. "Deal."

Chapter 4

Preparation was always key in this kind of investigation. Her abilities might be subjective, even instinctive, but there was a method to the madness. After working with so many ghost hunting teams, Ashlyn had learned the truth most people missed: there's a lot of waiting, and a lot of data collecting.

On TV, it all gets packed into an hour. Cut to the EMF spike, cut to the shadow down the hallway. Drama, jump scares, resolution. But in real life? You sit in the dark, wait, and sometimes reset batteries to check for cold spots that don't show up again. Then, you wait some more.

The part people talked about less was the emotional baggage. Hauntings didn't just happen in random places.

They clung to grief, fear, rage and love. All those big, raw feelings soaked into walls, stewing over centuries. That kind of energy could wear a person down, especially a medium with empathic tendencies like hers. Energy was still energy. Just because someone had been dead for two hundred years didn't mean it didn't hit like a freight train.

This was what she appreciated about Rhys. He didn't try to fix or downplay it. He understood what it felt like to carry other people's grief, alive or not.

A small flush rose on Ashlyn's neck. She'd never said she loved him, but she loved that about him, and that was close enough to be unsettling. Letting people in wasn't something she did easily. Other people's energy could be overwhelming, especially for someone like her. And Rhys? He felt everything too. That kind of connection had the potential to go very badly... or very, very right.

She picked up her phone, hesitated, then typed:

Doing my first night of investigation. Wish you were here. This one feels personal. Will update after tonight. I'll try to stay grounded.

He was probably asleep, UK time, but then again, he might be on a case of his own. Rhys had a way of surprising her when she least expected it. The screen stayed blank. She sighed, put the phone on her nightstand, and returned to her task.

Zac was green, but based on what she'd read in those Reddit forums, at least he'd done his homework. He'd also seen her on a few shows, so he knew her work as she presented on the screen.

She laid out the gear for them both: EMF reader, voice recorder, her field notebook. For Zac, she added a small protective charm, nothing fancy, just a little token from an earlier case, already soaked with intention.

For herself, she reached for the labradorite necklace, the one with the thumb-worn edge and faint blue shimmer. She slipped it over her head and let the stone settle against her collarbone. Then, she took out her notebook to gather her thoughts.

Onita was a young Seneca woman who was described as quiet, proud, sharp-eyed. Both Henri and Jean-Claude had been captivated by her. Did she choose Henri? There was nothing definitive, but the pieces pointed that way.

Jealous Jean-Claude instigated a drunken duel. Henri falling, maybe unconscious? Jean-Claude, in a panic, finishes the job, then tries to dismember him and get rid of the body.

The stories say he was interrupted with no time to clean up properly. He tosses Henri's body down the well and runs off with the head, wrapped in a castle tablecloth.

Ashlyn underlined that part in her notes. Legends had a way of evolving. They were passed down, retold, embellished. A detail added here, a shadowy twist there. Stories got spookier over time, but that didn't mean they were untrue.

Then there were the things she'd experienced. Her dream, the scraping noise echoing through the stones, and Naomi's ponytail lifting.

She flipped to a clean page and started a section labeled: Speculation.

— Blood moon: coincidence or catalyst?

— Is Naomi a descendant of Onita?

— Is this haunting a trauma still unresolved?

— Why now? Why here?

— Why does it feel intelligent, not just residual?

She drummed her pen on the rim of her notebook. The last light of day seeped into dusk, and outside the fort walls, the lake had changed to slate grey, rippling under a thin sheet of mist; the air felt charged, like that quick energy that builds just before the storm. It was almost time.

Ashlyn clasped the notebook, slipped it into her satchel, and stood on the edge of the bed, wondering if she should plunge back into more prep, but then she felt it: the slightest shift of space. Zac.

His energy had a bright, somewhat chaotic resonance, laced with some nervous excitement, like someone moving through a violent thunderstorm with a metal umbrella, and not knowing whether to feel terror or thrill. Just then, her phone buzzed on the nightstand.

Outside your door. Ready when you are.

She opened the door to find him standing there, backpack slung over one shoulder, flashlight in hand, with that eager-but-trying-not-to-be-too-eager expression.

"You look like you're ready to be in an episode of Scooby-Doo," she said with a wry smile, stepping aside.

Zac laughed as he brushed past her into the room. "Only missing the Scooby-snacks."

She shut the door behind him and turned to the table.

"Here," she said, handing Zac the EMF reader and voice recorder. Then she pressed the charm into his palm. "This is just a ward. Nothing fancy, just good energy. Keep it in your pocket."

Zac studied it, then tucked it away.

Outside, the night sky was a dim slate gray, and the air hung thick with humidity. They stepped into the courtyard together, heading toward the shadowed outline of the French Castle.

"First rule," Ashlyn said, breaking the silence, "don't talk during EVP sessions. I know it's tempting, but a single word, even a whisper, can affect the playback."

Zac nodded, serious. "I'll keep the commentary out of it. All mute, got it."

Ashlyn smirked. "And if something actually happens, like cold spots, a strange feeling, or just nagging existential dread, just tap my arm or raise your hand."

Zac did a little hand flexing at his side. "Understood."

They walked a few more steps until he added, "You've done this a lot, huh?"

"Definitely," she breathed. "But every place is different. Every haunting has its own rhythm."

Zac looked over at her, a little more serious now. "Do you ever get used to it?"

Ashlyn stopped to think. "Not really. But you learn how to hold steady."

"I can do that."

She stole a glance at him. His nervous energy had simmered down a bit and settled into something more focused. She was pleasantly surprised to discover that he was so adaptable.

"Good," she said. "Because no matter what happens tonight, we listen first. Then we respond."

Ashlyn tried to keep her steps slow and measured, while maintaining a steady breath. Every few feet they'd pass a lantern casting a dim yellow light, but the fog made it feel far away.

Zac walked just ahead of her, the old keys jingling in his pocket. When they reached the entrance, he turned back to her. "Are you sure about starting at the well?"

"That's where it all started," she said. "Might be where it wants to end."

He gave a small nod, then unlocked the door. The heavy wooden frame groaned as it opened, releasing a cold gust of air that smelled of stone and age-old cedar wood.

Inside, it was even quieter. They crossed through the shadowed passageway and emerged into the central courtyard, its flagstones black under the cloudy night. The sealed stone well stood nearer to the central opening, a behemoth set of weather-worn stones encircled with rusted iron.

Ashlyn stopped a few feet from it, her hand resting on her satchel. The energy was different here.

"Let's set up the recorder. This is where we start."

Zac crouched down next to the well as he carefully extracted the small digital audio recorder from its case. His hands were clumsy, but he balanced the recorder a flat stone that rested near the scaled rim of the well, angling the microphone off towards the open courtyard.

Ashlyn knelt next to him, observing. "Just make sure it's level. Even a slight angle will catch wind noise and make the recording will sound like a whisper."

Zac adjusted it, then sat back on his heels. "Like that?"

"Good enough for ghosts."

He gave a half-laugh to shake off nerves. Ashlyn stood and looked out into the fog-heavy dark.

"Ready?" she asked.

Zac inhaled as if he were about to dive underwater. "Not even a little."

Ashlyn smiled. "Perfect."

They sat in silence for a long time, with nothing. The EMF reader stayed still, the screen empty. Ashlyn didn't feel anything either, not even that familiar buzz at the edge of her senses. She asked her questions quietly, pausing after each one, then played the recording. Nothing but ambient static. Zac stayed silent beside her.

Ashlyn exhaled and adjusted her posture, letting her shoulders relax. If the usual approach wasn't working, she needed to shift gears. She closed her eyes and eased herself into a light, meditative state. Her breath became her anchor, guiding her inward, to the space where impressions stirred.

When the EMF reader beeped, she didn't flinch, just opened her senses a little wider. Out of the corner of her awareness, she felt Zac raise his hand. She gave a small nod, eyes still closed and waited. Something was coming.

Then it hit. Pressure settled against her chest, and her pulse slowed while everything tilted.

She saw the duel from the shadows. Henri was laughing, flushed with wine, circling with his sword raised in a show of bravado. The blur of motion came quickly, a misstep, a slip, and then the sharp, sickening sound of his head striking the stone.

Jean-Claude stood over him, breath ragged, sword dragging behind him with a low metallic scrape that echoed across the flagstones. Henri stirred. There was a hesitation before Jean-Claude drove the blade straight into his chest.

Ashlyn gasped, but the sound wasn't hers. It came from within the vision itself. Onita had witnessed it all, hidden and unable to stop it.

Jean-Claude couldn't see her. He moved fast, rushing into a nearby storeroom. He yanked a linen tablecloth from a shelf and spread it hastily on the ground near the well. At first, he tried to sever Henri's arm; the blade bounced off bone. Frustrated, he shifted his grip and went for the neck. The sawing was violent.

He placed the severed head atop the cloth, blood pooling quickly across the fabric. For a moment, he hesitated, then lifted the sword again, as if to return to the arm, but laughter spilled from upstairs. The party was winding down.

Jean-Claude's panic spiked. He grabbed Henri's limp body by the shoulders and dragged it to the well, shoving it over the edge. The splash was loud and didn't fade right away. Then he gathered the cloth-wrapped head and fled into the darkness. Onita followed.

Ashlyn came out of the trance, disoriented, her breath ragged. She blinked hard, her eyes struggling to refocus.

Zac was watching her, wide-eyed. "Hey. You okay?"

Ashlyn nodded, but it took her a second to find her voice. "Yeah," she said. "Just... needed a second."

She reached for her notebook with hands that didn't quite feel like her own yet and flipped to a fresh page, letting the words come without thinking too hard.

Henri fell. He wasn't dead. Jean-Claude made sure of that. She paused, pressed her palm to the page as if she could ground herself through the paper. Onita had seen everything.

Zac stayed quiet beside her, letting her work through what she'd seen. Ashlyn sketched slowly, rough outlines coming to life on the page. Henri's uniform, the way he'd fallen, the sword dragging behind Jean-Claude. She drew the well's iron rim; the tablecloth spread across the floor, and last, the eyes.

After a long silence, she looked over at Zac. "That wasn't just a vision. That was a memory."

He met her gaze. "You mean, like... from the land? Or from you?"

"Onita," she said.

Zac swallowed, but didn't look away. "Then we'd better keep listening."

A sudden noise broke the stillness, the scrape of metal, drawn out and unmistakable.

Zac stiffened. "Did you hear that?" he whispered.

Ashlyn turned her head toward the far wall, listening. "Yeah," she whispered. "That was real."

They stayed still a moment longer, letting the silence settle again. Then Ashlyn reached over and clicked off the recorder. "Let's see what we've got."

Zac remained still as she rewound the tape. Ambient hiss, her voice, asking questions, silence, and then—

There was an unfamiliar voice. It was soft, warbling, almost a pleasant singsong, but all wrong.

It was as though a man were trying to talk like a woman. Almost dramatic. It did not match anything she had felt or sensed within the vision. This wasn't a spirit; it was an act.

"That's not right," she said. "Certainly not what I connected with."

Zac looked jumpy. "You think it's fake?"

Ashlyn had stood up and scanned the area, her senses alive. "Let's find out."

They worked slowly, following a path around the perimeter of the main floor area. Zac crouched near the west wall, right under the broken wooden panel, and pointed. "Here."

Ashlyn knelt beside him, surprised how fast he had found something. It was a little device, cloaked in shadows, with a battery pack, PR speaker, and what looked like an old remote sensor. Someone had left this.

"Well," she exhaled. "There's your act."

Zac snorted, and his face was a bright shade of red. "But why would they go through all this work to fake something here? This place is already haunted."

"That's what I don't like. This feels like misdirection."

Ashlyn coiled the last of the audio cable, the false EVP still echoing in her ears. It had sounded wrong. She glanced again at the planted device wedged behind the panel: a cheap speaker, a battery pack, and a tangle of wires that looked like a rushed science project. Sloppy, but deliberate.

Zac had been standing beside her, slightly unsteady. "So… this means it was planted, right? Someone wanted us to find it, or at least, hear it."

"Or both," Ashlyn murmured. She bent back down, looking over the setup with a trained eye. "Whoever did this wasn't just screwing around; it simulated a haunting. They likely thought no one would check too closely."

Zac shifted his weight, head swiveling to look at the corners in the room. "Think there's more?"

"Maybe. We can do a sweep here in the morning when there is more light."

Ashlyn stood up, then slung the satchel over her shoulder, all her muscles stiff and aching from all the stillness of the vigil, while her mind swirled. The encounter, the vision, the presence, the tension in her chest had felt so strong, but this? This was something entirely different. A lie on top of the truth. It didn't make sense.

When they stepped out into the courtyard, Zac breathed out sharply. "Well… tonight was a lot."

Ashlyn nodded. "Yeah. And it is not over. We need to give Megan a heads up."

Zac blinked. "Now? It's pretty late."

"She's the program director," Ashlyn said, her tone even. "If someone is tampering with the site, especially before a public event, she needs to know. This isn't just a ghost story anymore; it's sabotage."

Zac pulled out his phone. "Alright. Should I call?"

"No," Ashlyn said after considering for a second. "Text. Let her sleep, but note it. She can decide in the morning."

Zac typed out a text while Ashlyn allowed her eyes to linger back at the view of the towering silhouette of the French Castle. In silence, she perceived the echo of earlier: the well, the vision, the eyes. There had been a real haunting, but now something else was stepping on its toes.

As they turned away, Ashlyn slipped out her notebook and jotted another note underneath the observations of the day:

Real or fake, something wants to be seen, and something else wants to be believed. She snapped the notebook shut as they stepped off into the dark.

Chapter 5

Ashlyn shifted in bed, staring at the ceiling while her mind refused to settle. Everything she'd experienced over the last twenty-four hours kept looping in her thoughts, and there were too many pieces that didn't fit together.

The vision at the well had felt real. So had the dream. Furthermore, the presence that seemed to cling to Naomi wasn't imagined. Ashlyn trusted her instincts, especially with the line between the living and the dead, but now, the planted ghost sounds and the staged equipment suggested someone was manipulating things.

She wasn't used to feeling this uncertain. The facts and the feelings didn't match, and that discrepancy left her uneasy. Was someone trying to undermine her? To make her doubt what she'd seen? She had never been one to jump to conclusions, but something about this case was different.

She rolled over and looked at the clock. 2:21 a.m. It was just past 7 in London, but Rhys might be awake. He often kept strange hours, especially when he was working.

Ashlyn picked up her phone and typed out a simple message:

You up?

Almost immediately, the screen lit with an incoming call, and she answered without hesitation.

"Hey," Rhys said, his voice soothing.

Hearing him speak brought a familiar sense of calm she hadn't realized she needed, and she let that feeling wash over her.

"You there?"

Ashlyn let out a slow breath. "Yeah. I'm here."

"Didn't expect to hear from you this early," Rhys said. "But I'm glad you did."

Ashlyn sat up, pulling the blanket around her shoulders. "I couldn't sleep."

A pause stretched between them.

"Do you want to talk about it?" he asked, "or just... not be alone with it for a bit?"

"I don't know what I need," she admitted. "Everything's a mess. There is definitely a haunting here; I've felt it., but there's also someone tampering with it, and I don't know where the line is anymore."

Rhys didn't rush in with reassurance or doubt. She rubbed her thumb along the seam of her blanket. "I'm used to sorting it out by feel. That's how I work, but this time... it's like someone's deliberately trying to make me second-guess myself."

"Maybe they are," he said, "but that doesn't mean they're succeeding."

Ashlyn closed her eyes. "It feels like they are."

"Alright," he breathed. "Then let's sit with that for a bit. You don't have to be certain tonight."

She let out half a laugh. "You always do that."

"Do what?"

"Remind me I don't have to fix everything all at once."

"You don't," he said. "And just because something is messy doesn't mean it isn't true."

Ashlyn rested her head back against the wall. "Thank you."

"For what?"

"Answering, listening, and not telling me, I'm imagining things."

"Never," Rhys said. "Not with you."

The silence that followed was softer than before. Not empty, just full of things that didn't need to be said out loud.

"I'll try to sleep again," she said after a while.

"I'll be here if you need me," he replied. "Even if you don't know why."

Ashlyn smiled. "Morning, Rhys."

"Goodnight, Ash."

Ashlyn ended the call and set the phone back on the nightstand, letting herself sink into the quiet. The doubt lingered, but it wasn't as loud now. Sleep came slowly, pulling her down in uneven layers. Fleeting images, muffled voices, and shadowed impressions pulled at her senses, but they faded as her breathing deepened and her thoughts dulled.

She didn't know how long she'd been asleep when the scream tore through the silence. Ashlyn sat up, alert, her heart slamming against her ribs. Another cry followed, louder this time, and unmistakably Naomi.

After kicking off the covers, Ashlyn hit the floor running, snatching the quartz from the nightstand on her way to the door. She yanked it open and stepped into the hallway, the stone cool against her bare feet. From somewhere down the corridor, footsteps echoed, heading her way.

There was no ghostly presence, only intense emotion. Ashlyn, though known for her connection to the past, could sense more than spirits. She had honed her sensitivity, often feeling things from far away. This time, the emotion was unmistakable: fear, and it was heading straight toward her.

A moment later, Naomi rounded the corner and collapsed into her arms. Ashlyn caught her, wrapping both arms around the woman and letting calm, grounding energy pulse outward.

Naomi inhaled, then exhaled in long, uneven breaths. Her heart pounded against Ashlyn's chest, then gradually slowed.

"I'm here," Ashlyn whispered.

In the distance, she heard footsteps pounding, then faltering. They paused, turned and moved the other way. Very human. The air still shimmered with something hot, like passion or entitlement.

Naomi tensed, then pulled back from the embrace, and Ashlyn studied her with care. A few scrapes on her palms. A mark already darkening on her upper arm that was shaped like fingers.

"You okay?" she asked.

Naomi gave a sharp nod. "I will be. Just startled, that's all."

Ashlyn didn't press. She knew enough about Naomi to recognize the deflection.

"What happened?"

Naomi hesitated, eyes flicking toward the courtyard. "I was warming up. I practice yoga most mornings before the others arrive. It clears my head."

Ashlyn waited, silent.

"I was in the middle of breathwork when someone grabbed me from behind." Her voice stayed level, but her hands curled in her lap. "I dropped low, kicked out hard and broke free, but they caught my arm before I ran."

She raised it, revealing the red, mottled imprint of a hand. The bruising had already bloomed in dark shades of purple and blue.

"They were wearing a ski mask," she added, "but I didn't stick around to study them."

Ashlyn studied the bruise on Naomi's arm. "Does it hurt?"

Naomi gave a dismissive shrug. "I'm anemic. I bruise easily. It looks worse than it is."

The pieces were already shifting. This wasn't random.

Ashlyn met Naomi's gaze. "It's not nothing. We need to call Megan. And maybe the police."

"No police," Naomi said quickly.

Ashlyn raised an eyebrow. "We can start with Megan."

Ashlyn led Naomi into the small room, where Naomi sank into the corner chair, her posture taut. Ashlyn grabbed her phone and dialed.

Megan picked up on the second ring. "Ashlyn," she said, "please tell me it's not getting worse."

"Did you see my text from last night?"

"I did. And I don't like it. I already called the police, just to get it on record, but they said there's not much they can do unless someone gets hurt. Apparently, 'faking a ghost' isn't a crime. They offered to come by around 10 to take a statement."

"Well, things just crossed the line," Ashlyn said, her voice low.

She looked over at Naomi, who sat silent, her shoulders rigid.

"Someone grabbed Naomi this morning. She got away, but she's shaken. There's a bruise on her arm, a clear handprint."

A long pause. Then Megan's controlled voice said, "I'll be right there, and I'll follow up with the police again. If this is turning into assault or harassment, they'll have to take it seriously."

Not long after Ashlyn made the call, Megan arrived, and right behind her came a man Ashlyn recognized from the field the day before. He carried two steaming paper cups.

He handed one to Naomi, who accepted it with a quiet nod of thanks. Ashlyn noticed how her fingers curled around the cup, as if she needed its warmth for more than just comfort.

"This is Marcus," Megan said, a little brighter than usual. "He's one of our longtime re-enactors who has been with us for years. Honestly, we'd be lost without him. He's always the first to volunteer and the last to leave. Works construction during the week, and has helped with sets too. Makes time for the fort every summer. Total lifesaver."

Marcus smiled, humble but aware of the praise. "Happy to help. I was in the break room when Megan got your call," he said, then turned to Naomi. "I'm so sorry this happened to you."

His voice was gentle, concerned, even, but Ashlyn watched the interaction. Something in his tone didn't sit right. It felt...rehearsed. The lines were all in the right place, but the energy beneath them was off.

Still, Naomi didn't flinch like she did in the yard. "Thanks, Marcus. I'm okay."

He took a step back, hands clasped in front of him. "I can start the morning drill if you need a moment," he offered, looking at Naomi and Megan.

"I already called Zac," Megan said. "He's on site too."

At that, Marcus stiffened just enough for Ashlyn to notice. His jaw twitched.

"What's he doing here this early?" he asked, the friendly tone slipping.

Megan blinked, surprised. "He has been helping Ashlyn with the archive and the investigation and came in to get an early start. Why?"

Marcus shrugged, but it didn't look casual. "No reason. Just... thought he usually came in later. I didn't realize he was that involved."

Ashlyn tilted her head, filing that away.

Naomi didn't speak, just took another sip of tea and kept her eyes low.

Ashlyn caught Megan's brief flicker of confusion, and then looked back at Marcus, who was watching Naomi a little too closely. Something was off.

"I need to get some paperwork done," Megan muttered, rubbing her temples, "and seriously consider canceling this event..."

"Don't do that," Naomi interrupted. "I know how much we need the income from this."

"Not at the expense of people getting hurt."

Megan turned to Ashlyn. "Will you meet Zac in the yard? I'll need both of you for the statement. You too, Naomi."

Naomi nodded, the tea still cradled in her hands.

"I'm going to take Naomi out for breakfast off-site before that," Marcus said.

He didn't ask; he declared. Naomi did not indicate that she cared. Her expression was unreadable. Maybe she was still in shock, or just too tired to argue. Either way, it didn't sit right.

As Ashlyn stepped out into the morning, the courtyard was not yet in full swing. She spotted Zac near the equipment tent, squatting with a crate and fiddling with a tangle of cords.

"Hey," she called.

He looked up and offered a sheepish grin. "Morning. Sorry I didn't come to check in when I heard about Naomi. I wiped it out in the yard. A tarp caught on something underfoot, and boom. Classic me."

Ashlyn's gaze dropped to his leg. He was favoring one side, a slight limp noticeable as he stood.

"You okay?"

"Yeah, yeah. Just bruised my pride," he said with a wince.

She gave a small smile, then her tone shifted. "Marcus is here with Naomi."

Zac's expression darkened. "Of course he is."

Ashlyn raised an eyebrow. "You don't like him."

"Is it that obvious?" Zac blew out a breath. "I just... don't trust him. He walks around like he owns the place. Naomi's polite about it, but I've seen the way he hovers."

"He's taking her out for breakfast."

Zac blinked. "Did she say that?"

"No, he did."

Zac rolled his eyes. "Classic Marcus. Pushy as hell when he thinks he's being charming."

Ashlyn looked at him. "You think he'd go as far as faking hauntings?"

Zac hesitated. "Honestly? I wouldn't put it past him. He's an attention whore."

Ashlyn crossed her arms. "He also seems to be a little interested in where you are."

Zac frowned. "What?"

"He asked you if you arrived early, a little too pointed."

Zac looked away for a second, then back. "Well, I guess I ruined his plan to be the knight in shining armor."

Ashlyn's gaze lingered. The limp, the timing, the attitude, all lined up in a way that made Zac look suspicious. Almost too perfect. And that, more than anything, made her uneasy.

Before long, more and more re-enactors arrived, and the yard was filled with movement. With Naomi off-site and Marcus conveniently choosing to accompany her, the typical tranquility that accompanies barrack drills was shattered. Everyone's gaze shifted to Zac as he moved into the center of the yard. Clipboard in hand, he looked a little out of place in his hoodie and shorts.

Ashlyn was near the outer wall, watching as Zac cleared his throat and lifted his voice just enough to break through the conversations happening around him.

"Alright everyone, Naomi is off site but will be here later. We will run a light warm-up today, just basics."

A few nods and murmured okays.

"Afterward, you will work with Keller on the volley timing. Also, make sure you check your dummy loads before we even think about touching the barrels. I mean it."

The re-enactors got a chuckle out of that, and one guy gave Zac a half-hearted salute.

"Camp followers and civilians - you will be with Evelyn at the north end of the grounds. She will walk you through a movement pattern, and where you stand during the market scene. If you are new, just follow her."

Zac looked at the clipboard for a moment before saying, "No live fire this morning, Megan's orders. I'll be around. Just message me if you need something."

It wasn't Naomi's commanding calm, but it sufficed. The groups broke apart and drifted to their designated areas.

Ashlyn walked across the grass to Zac as he stepped away from the center.

"You did well," she said, giving him half a smile.

He exhaled with relief. "They didn't throw tomatoes, so I'll take the win."

"Looks like practice is all set. Ready to go chat with the police?"

"Lead on," Zac grumbled. They walked together, and the rehearsal sounds drifted away.

By the time they made it to the admin wing, Megan's office had been transformed into a makeshift interview room. The chairs had been adjusted, one closer to Megan's desk, and one like a waiting area in the corner. A uniformed officer was positioned by the window, arms crossed with a notepad, though his expression was unreadable.

Ashlyn moved into the corner and gave Megan a quick nod.

Megan looked up from her paperwork, clearly thankful but tired. "Thanks for coming to get Zac," she said.

Naomi was the first to give her statement. She sat up straight in the guest chair, as the officer prompted her through typical questions. Her voice was level and moderate, but every word felt tight.

"I didn't see their face," Naomi stated. "They had on a ski mask. Black. Generic."

"And you said they grabbed your arm from behind?"

"Yes. I kicked backward, hard. I caught them in the shin or knee; I don't know which. That gave me just enough space to break away."

"Did they say anything? Make any sounds?"

Naomi paused. "No. Just breathing. Nothing else."

When the officer thanked Naomi, she stood, stepped aside, and did not say a word.

Marcus was next, with the same air of confidence as before. He nodded towards Megan, smiled at Ashlyn politely, and when he sat down, Marcus opened his arms a bit - he looked like he was just sitting down for a casual chit chat instead of a police interview.

"I was in the break room," he said, "grabbing a cup of coffee. I heard Megan talking to someone on the phone. She said that Naomi had been attacked. I ran right over."

Ashlyn stared at his hands. There was no fidgeting going on. His voice didn't waver. When the officer asked Marcus if he'd seen Zac that morning, the officer's gaze drew slightly.

"I think I saw him earlier than usual." He said. "Out back in the yard. Couldn't say for sure. Didn't really talk to him."

Ashlyn squinted.

After Marcus left the room, Zac was the next one called in. He was now noticeably limping and was slightly favoring a leg as he ambled around the room.

Ashlyn observed the officer casting his glance down, noticing the limp.

Zac told the officer where he had been, what he was doing, and how he had tripped over a tarp.

"I didn't hear anything," he added, "but I wasn't far, maybe 100 feet from the courtyard."

It was clear he was uncomfortable. He wasn't really being defensive, just nervous, like he wanted so badly not to say the wrong thing.

When he left the room, Ashlyn turned to Megan.

"Do you think it could have been him that attacked Naomi? Zac, I mean?"

Ashlyn shook her head. "I don't know. I've seen a lot of people lie, and I've seen scared people. He read, scared. Not guilty."

Megan blew out a breath and leaned back in her chair, pinching the bridge of her nose.

"Do you think this is ghost-related? I mean honestly. I'm juggling police reports and event permits - I have half a dozen actors threatening to walk. If this is just a haunting—"

Ashlyn cut in. "It's not just a haunting."

Megan looked at her, brows raised.

"There's a spirit here. Possibly more than one. But they don't feel like this. This was human... Naomi getting grabbed. The live round in the musket, the planted EVP? That's someone living. Someone using the ghost story as a costume."

Megan looked away for a moment. "So, ghosts and liars. Great."

"They're entangled somehow," Ashlyn said. "And that's what makes this dangerous. The spirit, Henri, is reacting. Henri is not violent by nature, but he is emotional and thinks Naomi is someone he lost. Zac is a threat. Someone is feeding that chaos. Maybe on purpose, maybe not."

"Marcus?"

Ashlyn did not respond directly. "He knew Naomi had been attacked, and he made plans to take her off-site before he even knew what she wanted. That's controlling."

Megan sighed. "He's been around forever and volunteers all the time. He is a great help with gear and never says no to cleanup or tech stuff... I don't want to think he would do something like this."

"Sometimes the people who blend in are the ones to pay attention to," Ashlyn said. "Just watch."

Megan nodded. "I'll update the board. And... I will keep Naomi with me the rest of the day."

Ashlyn stood. "Let me know when the officers are finished. I will do one last check of the grounds, and after that, I have more research to do in the archives."

She stopped at the door and turned back toward the hallway Naomi went. Ghosts she could work with. It was the living that scared her.

Chapter 6

The archive room was muggy with late-summer damp and still air that stuck to your skin. Three oscillating fans worked overtime in a futile attempt to cut the humidity, whirring in an uneven rhythm. The overhead light buzzed, and papers curled at the corners on the long wooden table.

Zac sat across from Ashlyn, hunched over a half-open folder, his expression unreadable. He was unusually quiet.

"You okay?" Ashlyn asked, keeping her tone casual.

He shrugged and then exhaled through his nose. "Yeah. Just... a little bent out of shape that Naomi went out with Marcus this morning."

Ashlyn nodded. "I get that."

Zac hesitated, then looked up. "You want the entire history?"

"Sure," she said. "How long have you all known each other?"

"This is our third summer." Zac leaned back, eyes drifting to the ceiling fan that wasn't moving. "Naomi and I started the same year. Marcus has been here forever. He's one of those guys who hits on anything with two legs and doesn't already have a ring on it."

Ashlyn raised an eyebrow.

"That being said, he didn't pay Naomi much attention until he figured out I liked her." Zac's mouth tightened, the corners turning down in frustration.

"There's this celebration party we do every year after Living History Weekend. I told Marcus I was thinking about asking her out. I was working up the nerve, but when I got the guts, he'd already asked her to dance."

Ashlyn winced in sympathy. "Ouch."

"Yeah. I think he asked her out too, but she turned him down. I don't know the details. When I talked to her, she just seemed... over it. Said she was tired and wanted to go home."

"And this summer?"

"All business," he said. "She's been focused, not cold, but not letting anyone in. She always had a professional edge, but now it's like she's got armor on."

Ashlyn considered that. "Have you talked to her outside of the historical society?"

Zac gave a short laugh, more self-deprecating than bitter. "No. I teach middle school, so I'm buried during the year. Summers are my chance to be here full time. After what happened at the party last year, I didn't have the guts to reach out. Didn't want to make things awkward."

Poor sweet Zac. He had a heart like an open book and an earnestness that would get him bruised in a world full of men like Marcus. He might be a little awkward, but his energy fit someone like Naomi better.

Ashlyn tilted her head. "What does she do outside of this?"

"She waitresses at this little cafe in Lewiston, I think. Something low-key. She said once she liked the hours, gave her time for auditions, beadwork commissions, all that. She's not into the 9-to-5 grind. Doesn't trust it." He smiled faintly. "Said she'd rather be broke and honest than salaried and miserable."

That tracked. Naomi moved like someone who knew what she was willing to trade her time for, and what she wasn't.

Zac fell quiet again, fingers tracing the edge of a faded muster roll. Ashlyn didn't push. Somewhere in the distance, a door thudded closed, and a shadow flickered against the far wall as if someone had walked past, even though they were alone.

"Hey, look at this," Zac said, his voice breaking the stillness of the archive room. His eyes had that excitement she recognized, like a puzzle piece had just clicked into place.

He slid a document across the table. Ashlyn leaned over it, scanning the handwritten lines. It was a French military record of deserter listings from the garrison at Fort Niagara.

Zac tapped two names.

"Henri Le Clerc, here listed as missing July 1757," he said. "And further down... Jean-Claude de Rochefort, August. One month apart."

Ashlyn raised her eyebrows. "I did not know there were this many desertions," she said. "Look at this list."

Zac nodded. "It was right in the middle of the French and Indian War, two years before the British took control of the fort. A lot of chaos for sure, but I'm not sure why Henri and all these others deserted. It's strange."

"Do you have the quartermaster report? The one about the cleaning of the well?" Ashlyn asked. "Let's line these up."

Zac sifted through the folder, located a smaller ledger, and flipped to a folded page. He handed it over.

"August 3rd, 1757," he said. "Here it is—Excessive blood pooled at base of the central well. No rainfall. Cleaned. Notified Capt. Rochefort. No follow-up action taken."

Ashlyn wrote everything in her notepad, the timeline beginning to take shape.

• Late July 1757–Henri went missing

• August 3rd–Blood located and cleaned from around well

• Mid August–Jean-Claude goes missing

• August 1757–New record: "Bound body located at wood line. Impossible to identify."

• Additionally: "Woman seen outside perimeter last evening. No statement taken."

Ashlyn froze on that last line. It was almost written as an afterthought, as if a woman in the woods, alone at night, in a time of war, wasn't worth investigating.

"Onita didn't just see what happened. She may have ended it."

Zac looked up. "You think she killed him?"

Ashlyn's tone was soft. "If Jean-Claude killed Henri, and she saw it, or found out afterward... it makes sense.

Maybe she waited to find out if the French would punish him."

"She was Seneca," Zac said, leaning back. "If the French buried it, there wouldn't be justice through their system. She may have needed to take it into her own hands."

Ashlyn tapped her pen on her notebook, her gears turning. "And if she did... that could be the very reason Henri's ghost is still here."

Zac frowned. "Because she avenged him?"

"Because maybe he doesn't know," Ashlyn said. "Or maybe the way he died left something uncompleted. Ghosts don't linger because of closure."

Zac looked down at the paper again. "Do you think she was punished?"

"No record of it," Ashlyn replied. "Which could mean she was never investigated. Or she was never caught."

The archive room was otherwise quiet, an underlying buzzing surrounded by ghosts of ink and dust. Ashlyn turned the page once more.

The temperature of the archive room shifted at such a subtle pace that it might not have been noticed had Ashlyn not already been attuned to something deeper. The damp, stale air seemed still. She stilled too, waiting, pencil poised a hair above the edge of her notebook. Across the table, Zac looked up as well, confused.

Then a tightening sensation pressed in behind her eyes. Ashlyn's sight was blurred, but not quite enough to unseat her, just enough to wash away the edges of the present.

The image unfolded as if it had always been in her mind. A woman was walking at dusk. The sky above her was low and gray, and her long hair was loose around her shoulders, tangled with wind and sweat. Her hands were streaked with blood and damp soil, and the hem of her dress dragged against the earth. Behind her, the trees loomed close. From somewhere above, a rhythmic creak of rope shifting against bark.

Ashlyn didn't realize she'd picked up her pencil until the page was half-filled. Her fingers moved, sketching the outline of the woman's silhouette, the trees arching over her.

Zac leaned over the table, lowering his voice as if he felt the moment needed more care than a casual tone.

"That's the grove by the lake. Just west of the palisade. It's not included on the current tour at all. It used to be a trailhead, I think, before the rules were as strict on the grounds."

Ashlyn looked up from her sketch, her thumb still smeared in pencil. "Do any of the re-enactors go out that way?"

He shook his head. "No one does. It's peaceful and overgrown. It is too far from the main yard, and the staff doesn't route anyone through there anymore. I don't think the new volunteers even know it is there."

A beat of silence passed between them. Ashlyn's eyes returned to the image on the page and the woman she had just seen and felt.

"That's where we need to go next," Ashlyn said. "Whoever is tampering with the site, and faking hauntings or setting equipment, won't have touched it. They wouldn't even know it is there."

Zac hesitated. "You think it is connected to the well and Henri?"

Ashlyn didn't answer at first, but her hand remained in the notebook, fingers brushing the edge of the sketch as if it might slip away if she weren't holding on to it. "I think she's part of the story that hasn't been shared, and if she's reached out now, it's not by coincidence."

She stood and pressed the notebook to her side, already thinking of the lake breeze, dusk settling gently through the trees the way it had in her vision. "That's where she is," she said. "If we want answers, we go where no one else would bother to look."

Zac gave a quick nod. His face was hard to read, but he seemed on board. "Then let's go."

"Tonight, after dark. Same time as last night."

Ashlyn glanced at the clock on the archive wall. There were plenty of hours to kill before darkness fell, just not enough for her to feel comfortable sitting still.

"We've got time," she said. "Let's get some fresh air. Maybe circle back to the others. I need to touch base with Megan anyway."

Zac hesitated, then rose to his feet, brushing a layer of dust from his jeans. "Naomi is probably still working the schedule board near the parade field."

Ashlyn caught something heavy in his tone.

"You want to talk to her." It wasn't a question.

Zac didn't argue it. "I just... I think I've got to ask her something. About Marcus."

They exchanged looks. "Okay," Ashlyn said. "Let's go find her."

The air in the hall outside the archive was cooler, and the light breeze lifting through the open windows felt pleasant. As they moved into the courtyard, the buzz of the day was wrapping up. Costumes were being packed, props were being dragged toward the barracks, voices lowered with the sun spilling towards the lake.

Naomi was standing at the end of a folding table under the shade of a canvas awning, clipboard in one hand, a pen behind her ear, flipping through the day's rehearsal notes.

Ashlyn and Zac crossed at a measured pace, but there was an undercurrent to their movements that neither would say aloud. Naomi glanced at them when they approached, her expression unreadable, but she didn't move.

She sat her clipboard down and looked at each of them. "You've got that look," she said, regarding Ashlyn. "Like something has gone sideways."

"Something did. We'll fill you in, but—" Her eyes flicked toward Zac, then back to Naomi. "Actually, there's something he wanted to say first."

She stepped back a pace, not out of the conversation, but just enough to give Zac space. She turned and pulled out her phone and pretended to scroll, watching the screen without seeing it, her body still angled toward them. Close enough to keep watch. Far enough to let something real unfold.

Naomi didn't answer right away. She looked between them, Zac with his hands shoved in his pockets, eyes downcast, and Ashlyn holding her phone. Finally, she folded her arms.

Zac shifted his weight. "Can I ask you something?"

Naomi raised one eyebrow but didn't shut him down. "Okay..."

He exhaled. "Is there... anything going on between you and Marcus?"

Naomi's face didn't change, but her silence stretched long enough that the question landed hard. She looked out toward the lake before answering. "Why?"

"Because I need to know," Zac said, his voice quiet. "I'm not trying to push. But I'd never let anyone hurt you, or get in the way."

That got her attention. Naomi's posture eased, acknowledging the truth in his voice. She met his eyes. "There's nothing. Not now. Not ever."

Ashlyn kept her head down, but her ears were still very much tuned to the moment. She didn't want to interfere, but she was rooting for Zac. Instinct made her glance toward the far end of the field.

Marcus was standing there, half in shadow beneath the edge of the barracks overhang, watching Naomi like someone memorizing her. His eyes tracked her movements with something that felt practiced.

Ashlyn's breath caught, and the heat of the afternoon seemed to vanish. In her mind, it wasn't Marcus standing there anymore. It was Jean-Claude, face tight with jealousy, jaw clenched, hands curled like they were already wrapped around the hilt of a sword. That same expression, that same cold focus. Watching Onita as if she were owed to him.

Marcus turned before she could move, disappearing behind the corner of the building, but as he walked away, he whistled. A slow, strange melody. Ashlyn didn't recognize the tune, but it sent a ripple up her spine. Something about it felt wrong. Like hearing a lullaby hummed at the wrong speed.

She blinked and realized Zac and Naomi were both looking at her.

Naomi's voice was the one that broke the silence. "Ashlyn? Did you hear me?"

Ashlyn turned toward her, phone still clutched in her hand, heart thudding a little too fast.

"Sorry," she said, steadying her voice. "What did you ask?"

Zac gave a half-smile, but it was tight. "We were asking if you think... whatever you saw, if it was a memory. Or a warning."

Ashlyn glanced at her sketchbook, at the figure of Onita beneath the trees, the creaking rope drawn in a ghost of pencil lines above her head.

"I think," she said, "it might be both."

As soon as the conversation with Zac and Naomi settled, Ashlyn slipped away under the pretense of needing to follow up on notes. She didn't want to interrupt whatever might still unfold between them. Besides, she had her own conversation to manage.

She made her way through the staff wing, past the cracked stone archway and into the admin building, where the air smelled of toner and lemon-scented cleaner. Megan's office door was cracked open, and Ashlyn gave a quick knock on the frame before stepping in.

Megan looked up from behind her desk in the middle of a call. She held up a hand, then wrapped it up.

"Right. Yes. I'll send over the report. Thanks, Officer." A pause. "Appreciate the follow-up."

She hung up with a decisive tap and rubbed both temples with her hands. "Please tell me you have good news."

"Depends on your definition."

Megan sighed. "That's what I thought." She leaned back in her chair and gestured toward the visitor chair across from her desk. "Sit. You might as well find out the latest."

Ashlyn sat with her notebook in her lap.

"There was another incident this morning," Megan said in a flat tone. "One of the newer volunteers cut her palm on a busted powder horn that she swears she picked up before there were not any cracks. Nobody else was around. It was actually not supposed to be in the armory staging area at all."

Ashlyn frowned. "Was it real powder or prop?"

"Prop. But the horn was a real horn. Split open as though it had been scored." Megan waved toward her monitor. "I already filled out the accident report. She's okay, just rattled. But her parents were... not happy."

"Well, it could have been worse."

"The police were already on site taking statements about Naomi's incident, so they could put it in the ongoing report. Their recommendation was contradictory to what I imagined—'postpone the event until the investigation is complete...'" Megan did air quotes while saying it and leaned her elbows on the desk. "They can't prove sabotage, but are concerned about escalation. I am too."

Ashlyn caught Megan's eye. "I'm doing another one tonight. I can't tell you where yet... just that it won't be anywhere we've discussed. The fewer people know about it, the better."

Megan gave her a dubious look. "You're not going to do anything irresponsible, are you?"

"No more than usual," Ashlyn said with a half-smile. Then, her tone became more straightforward. "I need twenty-four hours. Just until tomorrow night. If I can't hand you something useful by then, do whatever you have to do. Cancel, reschedule, I don't care. Just do what you can to keep people safe."

Megan exhaled through her nose and stared down at her desk for a long moment, weighing her options.

"It's Wednesday," she said. "Opening day is Friday. That gives me one full day to scramble if we pull the plug. Cutting it close."

"I know."

Another long pause. Then Megan gave a reluctant nod. "Okay. You've got until Thursday night. After that, if I'm not convinced we're in the clear, it's off the calendar."

Ashlyn stood up. "That's fair. I will check in again tomorrow."

"Be careful," Megan said. "I don't want to lose my actors to ghosts and lawsuits in the same week."

Ashlyn nodded to her and turned to go. She paused in the doorway; her voice dropped a little.

"Thanks for trusting me this long."

"I don't know if it's trust," Megan mumbled as she reached for her Coke. "Might be desperation. But either way, I'll take it for now."

Ashlyn left the office, and the door clicked shut behind her. She glanced at her phone. It was getting close to dusk. Time to get ready.

She crossed the courtyard with the sky settling into a soft steel gray with the evening around the fort. The sharp angles of the stone walls of the fort caught the last of the light, bottlenecking it just long enough so that it could lend long shadows to the courtyard and bleed toward the center.

Groups of re-enactors had finally drifted off between the staff wing and home, with only the sound of their laughter and conversation now fading into the distance. Tables were half-full, canvas shades were folded back against their poles, and equipment bins sat closed and latched. The commotion of the day had faded, but Naomi was still in the field.

She stood in front of the schedule board, head bent down in front of her clipboard, the pencil moving in quick strokes. The collar of her jacket turned up on the breeze, and her braid brushed her shoulder. She finished the note and underlined it. Zac was nowhere to be found.

Ashlyn slowed her pace as she got closer to Naomi, trying to keep quiet now that a calm of the yard had settled in. Naomi did not look up right away, but her pencil froze mid-mark, acknowledging Ashlyn with no need to verbalize it. Then it moved again.

When Ashlyn reached the front of the board, Naomi glanced up, and they made eye contact.

"Don't stay too late," said Ashlyn.

"I just need to finish some notes," said Naomi in an even voice. "Then I'll pack it all up."

Ashlyn paused. "Zac and I are doing an investigation tonight; you're more than welcome to join us."

"I'll pass," she said, and for a moment Ashlyn saw something indecipherable in Naomi's expression before it smoothed over. "But thank you."

Ashlyn did not stick around. She faced the dormitory quarters again, boots crunching against the gravel path, breath stuck in her throat. Inside her room, the quiet felt amplified. She tossed the notebook onto the desk, paused, and sat. Her fingers flicked open the cover and leafed through pages until she found the one where she had mapped out the triangle that circled Henri, Jean Claude, Onita.

It no longer felt like history. She reached for the pencil again and made a new set of lines. Zac, Marcus, Naomi. She stared at the shape for what felt like a long time, then closed her eyes. Outside the window, a lantern flickered twice, not randomly.

"Are you trying to protect her, Henri?"

Her phone vibrated. She blinked, expecting to see a reply from Zac, but the screen was blank. Frowning, she opened up her texts and typed a quick message to him.

Are you ready?

After hitting send, she stood up, feeling claustrophobic. She told herself she just needed a walk to clear her head, to reset before night. Ashlyn stepped into the courtyard expecting silence, but not this kind. The quiet had teeth now. The table that Naomi had been working at was still there, untouched, with the clipboard still in the middle of it, but Naomi was gone. Ashlyn looked around with a slow turn, scanning the yard. Something wasn't right.

She glanced down at her phone again, thumb hovering over her last message to Zac. No reply.

Where are you?

A strange feeling planted itself in her gut. Something was wrong. Naomi would not have left her clipboard there, and Zac, who always got back to her quickly, had gone silent. That was when Ashlyn noticed a flash of light.

It flickered at the end of the old trail, just past the palisade; where the tree line became dense. The path that Zac had told her was long forgotten. It was a place one should not go without a reason.

She took a few steps toward the light, but then stopped, her instincts telling her to watch. Another light glowed within the mist, as if it had been waiting for Ashlyn to notice.

What if Marcus was trying to recreate the past? What if he saw himself as Jean-Claude, and he believed Naomi was some sort of Onita stand-in? Perhaps this wasn't merely an obsession. Or perhaps instead, Zac followed Naomi and simply tried to stop it. Ashlyn's thoughts were getting frantic.

There was still no reply from Zac. She would not rush in stupidly, not without being prepared, but she would go, with or without him.

She headed back to her room and grabbed her field kit, hands instinctively moving even as her thoughts tore through her mind. If someone had gone ahead, if Naomi had been lured away or Zac had followed her without notifying her, then a flashlight and intuition might not be enough.

The path to the grove was no longer just a historical footnote or a psychic impression. The triangle she'd sketched was taking shape in real time, unfolding around them with disturbing precision. She was part of it now, drawn into the pattern whether or not she liked it, and if she didn't act, whatever had happened to Naomi, and whatever was keeping Zac silent, might only be the beginning.

Chapter 7

Ashlyn Alden wasn't afraid of ghosts. People, however, were complicated, and if anything was going to hurt her tonight, it would be flesh and bone.

She had her field kit slung over one shoulder, her Maglite clutched in her right hand as she slipped out of the staff quarters and crossed the quiet courtyard. The night air was thick with humidity. Gravel crunched under her boots as she made her way toward the narrow path that led to the old grove beyond the palisade, the one Zac had mentioned.

She paused at the edge of the trees, thumb flicking across her phone screen. One last text to Zac.

This wasn't smart, and she knew it. Heading into the dark alone after someone who might or might not be missing? She'd made better decisions. Hell, she'd made worse ones too. But not knowing was worse than the risk.

With a quiet sigh, she opened a message to Rhys.

Doing something stupid. If you don't hear from me again, know I...

Her thumb hovered. Too dramatic.

She backspaced a few characters, then typed instead:

If you don't hear from me, call Megan Clarke at Old Fort Niagara, and tell her I followed the path outside the fort to the lake.

Then she hit send, locked the phone, and slipped it into her coat pocket.

The trees loomed ahead, and Ashlyn adjusted the strap of her bag, clicked on the flashlight, and stepped off the path and into the dark.

Before long, her senses kicked in, and the pressure behind her eyes spiked, a sure sign something was stirring. The air buzzed like static under her skin. This was more than just old trauma soaked into the soil. The grove was a hotbed of psychic energy, pulsing beneath like a heartbeat.

She stepped off the trail as it opened into a moonlit clearing near the lake's edge. The path ended abruptly, swallowed by tall grasses and damp earth, as if the forest had pulled back to reveal something sacred.

Above, the moon hung low, casting a cold silver glow over the grove. The lake shimmered beyond, its dark surface broken only by faint ripples. The air smelled of wet stone and old leaves. Near the center stood a lone tree, wide-trunked and gnarled, roots curling into the earth. Its bark was mottled with moss and lichen, and it leaned to the right, exactly as she'd drawn it.

This was the place from her vision she sketched. The one where Onita had walked away with blood on her hands. Crouched at its base, looking small and shaken, was Zac.

"Zac?" she called. Her voice was swallowed by the lapping of the lake.

He didn't look up right away, as if he was struggling to place the sound. One hand was braced against the bark, his fingers splayed as if the tree itself might hold him steady. His other hand was curled near his chest, trembling. Just beside him, his flashlight had rolled into the grass, still flickering like it couldn't decide whether to stay on or die out. The beam shone against the roots and cast long, distorted shadows that seemed to move on their own. He turned toward her as if waking from a dream.

"Ashlyn?" he rasped.

She was at his side in three quick strides, dropping to a crouch. "What happened?"

"I—I followed them," he stammered. "I saw Naomi come down the path. She was moving fast. I thought maybe she'd seen something, or maybe the spirit... I don't know. Then I saw Marcus; he was right behind her. I think he was chasing her."

He shook his head, eyes unfocused. "I followed them, but when I got here... they were gone."

"Gone?"

He nodded. "I didn't see or hear them. I checked around the grove, even down by the edge of the lake. Nothing."

She glanced toward the water, then back at him. The hair on the back of her neck stood up. "Zac. Are you sure it was them and not something else?"

He blinked. "What? Like Ghosts?"

"You're absolutely sure?" Ashlyn repeated, "That you saw Naomi and Marcus?"

"Yes," he said. "I think so."

"Zac," she said again, more firmly this time. "Look at me. You saw Naomi and Marcus?"

He opened his mouth, but the words caught. She watched as the moment doubt eclipsed certainty.

"I thought I did," he whispered. "I followed someone, and I was sure it was him."

Ashlyn's gaze drifted back to the tree, and her pulse quickened. The energy around here was still speaking to her, and the bark beneath Zac's hand seemed to swallow the light. This place was holding onto something, and whatever had drawn Zac here... wasn't finished. The grove went so quiet that even the wind had vanished. Something felt wrong.

Ashlyn stood, her flashlight sweeping across the tangled roots. Her breath caught as the beam paused on a shallow dip in the earth just a few feet away. Something stirred and she could almost remember a flicker of candlelight and a drop of blood blooming across white linen. This place had known death.

"Come on," she said, offering her hand to Zac. "We need to tell Megan. Now."

Zac looked up, pale and wide-eyed. "Ashlyn."

He gestured towards the dent in the earth. "Do you think that's where we're going to find the... head..."

She didn't hear him finish, and with her next breath, the world fell away. Darkness folded inward, and within it, something flickered into view.

Jean-Claude stumbled into the clearing, panting, his boots slipping in the damp earth. He was holding something against his chest, the linen cloth soaked through, tightly wrapped and dripping red. There was a shovel tucked under one arm, and his eyes darted, the look a mixture of panicked and grief-stricken.

He dropped to his knees by the roots of the tree and started digging frantically, the shovel biting into the damp earth with wet thunks. A voice broke the darkness.

"You killed him!"

Onita stood at the edge of the clearing, her form rigid, glaring with such rage.

Jean-Claude froze, then he turned to her.

"You don't understand," he said, voice breaking. "Henri was not what you thought."

Onita moved forward, furious and radiating heat. "He loved me!"

"No," Jean-Claude said. "He wanted to use you. Trade favors, secrets, for your trust. I tried to stop it."

His words collapsed, and Ashlyn could feel sorrow spiral through him, wrapped with guilt and something darker. The scene flickered at the edges, and the linen bundle slipped from Jean-Claude's hands, landing with a soft, final thud beside the half-dug hole. Ashlyn gasped as the vision broke, and she dropped back into her physical body.

"I think Jean-Claude buried the head here," Ashlyn said, dropping to her knees. She began digging at the earth with her hands. The dirt crumbled beneath her nails as she scraped, and her breath was coming fast and shallow.

"He ... seemed almost regretful. Like he really thought he was protecting Onita."

Zac knelt beside her and placed his hand on her shoulder. "Hey, it's been over two hundred years. Let's get some help. Or at least a shovel."

Ashlyn paused, hands still in the soil, and let out a deep breath.

"You're right," she said as the vision loosened its grip, her own thoughts asserting themselves once again. "This is why I don't like to do this alone. Sometimes the energy... the emotions... take over."

Zac glanced up from his phone with a sheepish grin. "Sorry I didn't text back. I think my emotions got the better of me too."

Ashlyn huffed a laugh, brushing dirt from her palms. "Yeah, well. Haunted forts and buried heads will do that to you."

She stood, wiping her hands on her jeans. "We need to find Megan. Let her know what we've seen. And text Naomi to make sure you actually saw her earlier, and it wasn't just the spirits playing tricks."

Zac's smile faded into something more serious as he tapped out a message on his phone.

Together, they headed back toward the main buildings. When they stepped into the administrative wing, the low hum of overhead fluorescents greeted them.

Megan was still in her office, hunched over her desk with a stack of forms that looked like they were multiplying.

She glanced up as they entered. "Please tell me you didn't find another cannon loaded with live ammo."

Ashlyn shook her head. "Not quite. But we may have found something. What are you doing here this late?"

Megan rubbed her eyes. "Trying to come up with a contingency plan in case we have to cancel Living History. We can't afford to refund all those tickets and keep the doors open."

Ashlyn nodded, reminded once again of the practical side of things. Money made the world spin, and without enough donations or grants, the fort relied on tourists to survive. Keeping history alive was important, even if sometimes we got that history wrong. As the thought passed through her mind, an idea formed, but she pushed it down for now, focusing on the task at hand.

"Zac saw Naomi and Marcus both head down the overgrown trail to the lake," she said. "But when we followed, they were gone. Like they disappeared."

Megan blinked, then shook her head. "What does that even mean?"

She exhaled. "I mean... I know what it means. But are you saying they're in on this? I don't buy it. Not even with

Marcus and his vanity. He loves the reenactments. He'd never do anything that—"

"Not necessarily anything like that," Ashlyn interrupted-ed.

"I was the one who followed them," Zac added. "Ashlyn followed me."

"When I got to the clearing in front of the lake, that's where I found Zac," Ashlyn continued. "And I had a vision. I think I may have found where the body, or at least the head, of Henri Le Clerc is buried. That spot might be the center of everything that's happening."

Megan's eyes narrowed, but her voice was calm. "I'm listening."

Ashlyn explained what Jean-Claude had said in the vision, that Henri wasn't who Onita thought he was, and how the vision had ended before she could hear Onita's response. There was more to uncover, she was sure of it, but the message felt unfinished. If she could find the skull, maybe it would offer another piece of the puzzle. Maybe even a way to reach them both again.

"But I don't know how I'd prove any of it," she admitted. "Even if I find it. A psychic impression isn't exactly court evidence."

"That's simple enough," Megan said, standing and stretching her back. "Zac should have the key to the grounds, and we've got shovels in the maintenance shed. Once I wrap things up here, I'm happy to help dig."

Ashlyn looked over at her. "Thank you," she said, then turned to Zac. "Have you heard anything? From Marcus or Naomi?"

Zac flushed. "I only texted Naomi, don't have Marcus's contact info... and nothing from her yet."

"I've got his number," Megan said, pulling her phone from her pocket. "and will call him. Naomi might just be working, maybe a late shift at the cafe."

Ashlyn frowned. "She was still on site when I saw her, maybe twenty, twenty-five minutes before Zac thought he saw her heading down the trail."

Megan's eyes darkened. "I don't like this one bit."

"Any luck finding out who planted the fake haunting at the well?" Ashlyn asked, her tone careful.

Megan shook her head. "Nothing yet." Then she turned to Zac. "Are you sure you actually saw them?"

Zac's posture tensed. "Of course I'm sure," he said, sharper than usual. "Why would I make that up? Naomi could be in real danger."

Megan held up a hand, guilt flashing across her face. "Sorry, Zac. You're right. I'm just... rattled. We'll find them both."

Zac nodded stiffly, but Ashlyn could tell he couldn't care less whether or not they found Marcus. His concern was for Naomi.

"Let's start with digging up the skull at the clearing," Ashlyn placed a hand on Zac's arm. "Megan will find Naomi."

They made it back to the clearing just after midnight, the woods dense with silence. The moon hung low behind a veil of thin clouds, casting a muted glow over the clearing. The air was cool, damp, and thick with the hush of something waiting.

Zac walked a few paces behind, quiet and withdrawn, his eyes fixed on the ground, and movements stiff. Whatever had shaken him earlier hadn't left; if anything, it had settled deeper.

Ashlyn stepped into the clearing and slowed. The tree stood as they left it, its roots tangled in shadow. She slipped off her pack and leaned it against the base of the trunk, and without speaking, she and Zac began to dig.

The ground was soft from recent rain, and the roots reached like veins through the soil. It didn't take long. Just under two feet down, Ashlyn's trowel struck something solid, and a sharp crack echoed through the clearing.

Ashlyn flinched, brushing away dirt with shaking fingers. There nestled in the loam was a broken piece of bone, an unmistakable fragment of a skull.

Zac crouched beside her, face pale. "Is that—?"

She nodded once, her throat too tight to speak. Together, they cleared the rest. Time had fractured the skull, but enough remained intact to piece it together. Ashlyn cradled it in both hands.

"Alas, poor Henri," she murmured, a bitter smile tugging at her lips. "I knew you... in theory."

Then she closed her eyes and exhaled, holding the head in her lap. The bones were cool and hummed in her mind. They had a story to tell. She let herself slip into the current.

The vision came fast. She stood in a stone hallway, torchlight casting wild shadows across the room. He was confused and angry. Jean-Claude stood opposite him, voice raised, words sharp.

"You betrayed us."

Henri blinked. "What are you talking about?"

There was no recognition in his voice. He tried to laugh it off, but Jean-Claude's eyes were wild with certainty.

The duel happened quickly. Faster than memory should allow. A slip, a crack of bone against stone, and then Henri was falling and darkness surged in.

It didn't end there. Henri's awareness flickered back on. Distant pain. Stone against his back. The scent of blood, and somewhere far away, Onita. She's in danger, he thought. Jean-Claude will hurt her. She doesn't know. I have to warn her, but he couldn't move or speak. Time swam and then he saw Jean-Claude, swinging in the trees. Rope taut, neck broken.

Ashlyn gasped as she came out of the vision, blinking at the skull in her hands. Henri wasn't a ghost out for vengeance. He lingered because he believed Onita was still in danger. He didn't know Jean- Claude would never have hurt Onita, but they were all here now, repeating the same story.

Footsteps crunched on the trail behind them. Ashlyn turned as Megan stepped into the clearing, phone in hand and a grim look on her face. Just behind her, Marcus followed with a smug look on his face (or maybe that was just his face).

"Look who I got ahold of," Megan said, voice tight. "Marcus was at home. Safe and sound. I called the cafe too... Naomi's not there."

Her gaze darted to Zac. "Could she have been with someone else with her?"

"I wanted to help," Marcus chimed in, his tone too smooth. "Was worried about Naomi"

Zac spun around, eyes wild as he stepped toward Marcus

"What did you do with her?" he snapped, closing the space between them and jabbing a finger at Marcus's chest.

Marcus narrowed his eyes, stepping closer, his face right up to Zac's

"I didn't do anything, man. You're the one who was with her; I was home."

Zac shoved him. "You're always hovering around her, acting like she owes you something!"

Marcus did not budge and laughed, just a little.

"She's a grown woman, Zac. Maybe she just wants a grown man."

Megan stepped between them.

"Enough! This isn't helping Naomi!"

Ashlyn flinched as the skull slipped from her hands and hit the dirt with a dull thud. Her breath caught, and the world narrowed to shadow and cold. Another vision seized her, harder and faster than the last.

She was running, no, moving with purpose through the forest, her feet sure beneath her. Two men flanked her, close and silent. Ashlyn knew them instinctively: Onita's brothers. This wasn't just a memory; it was a reckoning.

Underbrush whispered against her shoulders as she stepped into the clearing, the same one where Henri's skull now lay exposed in the present. Ahead, under the moon-light, Jean-Claude knelt at the base of the tree, digging.

His hands trembled as he worked. The linen-wrapped bundle beside him sagged with Henri's head.

"Why?" she demanded, stepping forward. Her voice was low.

Jean-Claude startled and rose, dirt smearing his coat sleeves. His face was pale, and not just by what he'd done.

"He betrayed us," he said. "He was passing information to the British. Using you to do it."

Lies. Or were they? Onita's heart didn't know what to believe. She had loved Henri, or wanted to, but the man before her had stripped that love away.

"I would never have chosen you," she said flatly. "Not before. And certainly not now."

Jean-Claude's jaw clenched, but he didn't plead. He looked at her brothers, then back to her, almost as if asking for a verdict. Onita signaled.

The brothers moved fast, one circling behind, the other slamming the butt of a musket into Jean-Claude's ribs, dropping him to his knees. He gasped, winded, but didn't resist.

This wasn't a brawl; it was an execution. They pulled him to his feet and marched him toward a low-hanging branch of the magnificent tree. A rope had already been prepared by Onita.

Jean-Claude looked at her, not pleading, just waiting as if he knew this was the only ending left. One brother slipped the rope around his neck. The other let him drop. His body fell, a single, jerking breath, then stillness. Not a soldier's death, a sentence, carried out.

Onita stepped forward as his boots twitched above the earth, then stilled. The silence was absolute.

"You took him from me," she said. "And no truth justifies that."

Ashlyn gasped as the vision tore away. The clearing lurched around her, and her knees gave out. She dropped hard to the forest floor, breath ragged, palms pressed to the earth like she was afraid it might tip her sideways.

"Ashlyn!" Zac was at her side in seconds, kneeling beside her. "Are you okay? What happened?"

Megan rushed forward too, crouching beside her. Even Marcus took a step closer, unease tightening his features.

"I'm fine," Ashlyn managed, though her voice was thin. "Just—give me a second."

Zac steadied her arm while she caught her breath. Her fingers trembled.

"They were all trying to do the right thing," she said. "That's why this hasn't ended."

The others exchanged glances, but she pushed herself upright, brushing dirt from her hands.

"The haunting persists because no one was fully wrong," she said more clearly now, standing. "But none of them were fully right either. Henri thought he was protecting Onita. Jean-Claude believed he was protecting her people. Onita… she stopped being someone's prize and became the judge."

She looked from one face to the next. "Now we're stuck here, playing out their grief over and over."

Marcus scoffed. "That's great and poetic, but how does it help us find Naomi?"

Zac turned on him, jaw clenched. "You don't get to say her name like that."

Marcus raised his eyebrows. "What, you think you're the only one who cares? You've been acting like some tragic lead ever since rehearsal. Get over yourself."

Zac stepped forward, furious. "I was trying to protect her!"

"And look where that got us," Marcus snapped.

"Stop it!" Ashlyn's voice cracked through the night like a whip. "This isn't about you. Either of you. It's not about who was right or who tried harder. It's about Naomi, who is still missing."

The clearing fell into a tense, loaded silence. Even the trees seemed to hold their breath. Ashlyn turned toward the woods, eyes narrowing as the wind shifted. The air had changed again. Something was moving out there.

"She's nearby," Ashlyn said. "I can't explain how, I just know."

She looked at each of them.

"Come on. We need to go before this place decides how her story ends."

Chapter 8

"Ashlyn, I don't like what you're saying," Megan said with a tight voice. "You're freaking me out."

Ashlyn didn't flinch. "There's a lot of unfinished business here. The kind that rots, and the psychic energy clings to this place. It's not just ghosts at this point. Zac saw both Naomi and Marcus walk into the woods, except we now know Marcus wasn't there. So, who did she follow?"

Megan's eyes went wide, but before she could speak, Ashlyn continued. "Also, someone has been purposely faking paranormal activity. Layering fake evidence over a real haunting. It's manipulative and reckless, and there's potential to lose more than just profit."

"Wait, what the hell are you talking about?" Marcus interrupted, his voice sharp. "A fake haunting?"

Ashlyn looked at him. "Yes. The other night, during our session at the well, Zac and I found planted equipment, disguised as paranormal evidence. A speaker was set up to play fake EVP with voices pretending to be dead people."

Zac shifted beside her, his arms crossed. "It was hidden behind one of the old wall panels. Timer rigged. Looked like someone wanted us to believe the ghost was a woman."

"Who would even do that?" Marcus scoffed, the corner of his lips curling into a smirk. "Sounds like a lot of drama to me."

Ashlyn narrowed her eyes. "Exactly. Someone who wants attention or control, or to make it so muddy that nobody knows what's real anymore."

Marcus barked out a short, humorless laugh. "Well, maybe that's your job, isn't it? Stir the pot to get everyone thinking this place is haunted so you can play psychic hero."

Zac stepped forward, annoyed. "She wasn't even here until after the haunting stuff started, and she's not making that up! I saw the gear myself."

Marcus was eyeing him for a minute. "Right. And we're just supposed to take your word for it now."

Zac had balled his fists at his side. "What's that supposed to mean?"

"I don't know," Marcus said, shrugging. "You're the one who said you saw Naomi and me go into the woods together, but I was at home, remember?"

Ashlyn stepped in between them. "Guys…"

The air was wound tight with accusation, and something even more sinister was festering beneath the surface. This fort wasn't just haunted by the dead; it was affecting the living.

"Enough," Megan boomed, cutting through the tension. She sounded like a tired mom trying to corral her misbehaving children. "Let's keep our focus on finding Naomi."

"Assuming you actually saw her," Marcus huffed under his breath.

Zac puffed up, but before he could speak, Megan shot Marcus a look, and he stopped talking, clenched his jaw and looked away.

"We need to split up," Ashlyn said, stepping forward. "We can cover more ground."

She unclipped a spare flashlight and handed it Megan. "You and Zac go up the interior trail, check out the area around the sheds and the tree line at the reenactment field.

Marcus and I are going to take the southern direction towards the woods."

Zac was cut off, his throat catching. "But-"

"I'll be okay," Ashlyn interrupted. "I am not in danger from Marcus."

Zac looked skeptical. His mouth tightened, but he didn't say anything. He just nodded once and turned to follow Megan, who was already walking through the darkness with her flashlight beaming a path.

Ashlyn spun without waiting for Marcus and headed toward the trees. He caught up after a few long strides and walked beside her.

The path below was more of a suggestion than a trail, but was softened by moss, pine needles, and time. They walked together for a minute in silence, flashlights flickering through the brush. Ashlyn let her senses open, wanting to sense the surrounding forest, not just visually, but with that energy that hummed behind her ribs.

"I still don't think she is out here," Marcus muttered, pointing his beam at a patch of brush. "She probably went into town or blew off some steam somewhere. Everyone's acting like she's been kidnapped."

Ashlyn hesitated. Her eyes were locked on the shadow up ahead, which seemed to shimmer a little too much in the corner of her vision.

She stopped, and Marcus almost ran right into her. "What's up?"

"She came this way," Ashlyn murmured. "I can feel it."

"You and your ghost radar."

Ashlyn ignored the jab and stepped off the path, brushing past a low branch. The slope of the terrain had been gradual, but now it dropped sharply as they followed the trail down towards the lake. They could hear the gentle waves of water brushing against the shore. Somewhere to their right, a bird took off, wings beating the air.

"Down there," Marcus said, pointing towards a break in the trees. "There's a bluff. Not huge, but she could have fallen and twisted an ankle or worse."

"Yeah. Let's check," Ashlyn responded.

They moved faster now, their pace matching the urgency of voices that were echoing behind them, faint but carrying through the woods.

"Naomi!" Megan called. "Naomi, are you there?"

Zac's voice soon followed. "Naomi! If you are out here, please say something!"

Ashlyn cupped her hands around her mouth and followed suit. "Naomi!"

Marcus called too, but his voice was flat and lacked conviction. The bluff should be just up ahead now, the trees thinning, the soft earth lightly clinging from the mist of the lake. To the right, maybe ten feet away from where they were standing, was a figure standing still underneath a tall tree.

"Naomi!" Ashlyn shouted, but the figure didn't move. "Hey, Marcus, do you see that?"

Marcus turned to where her eyes were locked.

"What the hell…"

She was a woman. Barefoot, with long dark hair hanging in damp ropes below her shoulders. Her dress fluttered in the breeze, accentuating her exposed arms.

"Naomi?" Marcus called again, even though he knew it wasn't.

Ashlyn stepped forward. The flashlight flickered, and then the figure was gone, as if it had evaporated into thin air.

"That was a powerful manifestation," Ashlyn whispered.

Marcus stiffened next to her. She could feel the fear emanating from him in waves.

"You okay?" she asked, her eyes glued to the place where the woman had stood.

"I think so." He muttered. "I've never actually seen a…"

"There," Ashlyn said, pointing to the base of the tree.

A scrap of fabric was fluttering against the bark, half caught in the roots. She broke into a jog, running to it, and then suddenly the ground dropped beneath her foot. Marcus grabbed her arm just as she stumbled, pulling her back sharply and they tumbled a few feet to the mossy ground.

"Jesus, Ashlyn!" he shouted, still holding her arm. "You almost went over!"

"I didn't see it. The edge just vanished."

Marcus let go and looked at the slope. "You could have broken your neck."

She didn't respond. Her gaze remained focused on the fabric.

"She was leading us."

Marcus lowered his voice. "Who was?"

Ashlyn stood, brushing off her pants. "Onita. The ghost."

She peered back down to the edge, her flashlight moving up and down the steep slope. The bluff probably wasn't over ten or twelve feet high, but the edge was jagged and rocky, with tree roots sticking out and damp leaves over the rocks and ground that made it dangerous. At the bottom, wedged beneath a clump of ferns, was Naomi. She was not moving.

"She's down there."

Marcus stepped beside her and shone his flashlight. "Shit. I think she rolled off the bluff."

Ashlyn took another scan. There was no sheer drop, but it was not a gentle hill either.

"I'm going down." Ashlyn moved toward the drop.

Marcus caught her by the arm. "We don't need you both hurt, or worse."

"I just need to see if she's breathing."

She clipped the flashlight to her belt and, with both hands free, crouched lower to test weight distribution. Left foot, then right foot, sliding her foot sideways for traction until she found a thin low branch to grab. Then she found one section of stone with enough support for her center to pivot and move to the next section.

Marcus also made a go of it, but even slower; she could hear him muttering a curse as a twig snagged his shirt. When Ashlyn reached the bottom, she dropped to her knees. Naomi was lying on her side; her left arm was curled near her chest.

She brushed away a few leaves from Naomi's face, only to discover a small gash on her forehead near the top of her hairline, while a bruise turning blue around her jaw.

Marcus circled them, snapping his flashlight down at them. "Don't move her. We don't know how bad it is."

Ashlyn nodded. "I won't. I am just checking."

She reached two fingers into Naomi's neck and found a slow, steady heartbeat. Relief spread through her chest. "Pulse is good."

Marcus knelt, inspecting her legs and arms from a distance. "I don't see anything broken. She may have fallen and bumped her head."

Naomi stirred then, just a twitch of her fingers, her breath catching on something painful.

"Naomi," Ashlyn said, brushing her knuckles against the woman's shoulder. "Hey. Can you hear me?"

Nothing.

"We need to get help," Marcus said, his voice sharper now, adrenaline overtaking the initial fear.

Ashlyn looked up at the bluff, then back down at Naomi's still form. "Call 911 first," she said. "Then text Megan and Zac. Let them know we found her."

Marcus already had his phone in hand. "On it."

He turned and dialed, pacing a few steps to get better service. Ashlyn could hear the faint conversation.

"Yes, Fort Niagara, wooded trail past the southern bluff. Yes, we have a woman down... head injury, unconscious but breathing... Yes, I will stay on the line."

He shot Ashlyn a quick glance and nodded. "They're dispatching EMS now. They said it might take some extra minutes because of the terrain."

Ashlyn exhaled. "Good. Now, text the others."

Marcus thumbed a text, then put his phone away and faced the incline.

"I'll climb back up and signal them," he stated, already moving towards the steep slope they had just come down. "You stay with her, just in case."

Ashlyn said nothing, but turned back, brushing away another pine needle.

"Help is on the way," she whispered, not only to Naomi but also to herself.

Up above, she could see the flashlight beam bobbing and weaving through the trees as Marcus scrambled up the steeper slope, his voice cutting through the night air.

"Zac! Megan! Down here, we found her!" Ashlyn heard Marcus moving over the dry leaves and underbrush away from them as he reached the top of the rise. For several moments, Ashlyn was alone again with Naomi.

The air felt laced with an undeniable psychic energy, like something unseen still lurked nearby, watching. She kept her hand near Naomi's shoulder, not touching, but hovering, tensing her muscles into a fixed position, and breathing in and out in a quiet meditation.

Then came the rustle of footsteps from above, and moments later, Megan's echoed voice bounced down the slope. "Ashlyn! Are you hurt? Is she —?"

"We're okay!" Ashlyn replied. "She's breathing, but she is out cold! EMS is on the way."

Zac's face appeared next, skidding down beside them, eyes wild with worry. "Oh God, Naomi...."

Slight pressure coursed through the space, felt by all. A shiver ran up Ashlyn's arms, Zac moved back, and Megan went quiet.

Then Naomi's eyes snapped open. Ashlyn gasped and dropped to her knees beside her just as Naomi's fingers pressed against the forest floor. She tried to speak, but what came out was not her voice. Her eyes didn't move, locked on something just beyond Ashlyn's shoulder.

Marcus. "Naomi?" he said, voice low. "Hey. You're okay."

Naomi didn't blink. Her lips moved again, slower this time, and her voice came clearer, but the cadence was off. It wasn't Naomi speaking; it was Onita.

She must have been channeling through Naomi's battered, psychically open body. Not a possession so much as a merging. A moment of clarity granted by sheer emotion and the thin veil of near-death.

Then, there was a sharp jolt from the pack. The EMF reader pinged, giving off a shrill, rising whine. Zac jumped, scrambling to unzip the bag and fumble it open, the device clicking frantically, the needle moving to the red.

"It's not even on," he whispered.

Megan cursed quietly as Naomi spoke.

"You killed him."

The tone of her voice was not panicked or confused, just measured. It did not belong to Naomi.

Marcus stopped, color draining from his face. "What?"

Naomi's brow furrowed, her breath steady and slow. "You took him from me," she said again. "I saw the blood."

Marcus swallowed rapidly, blinking. Then he steadied. The tension in his body slipped away, and his shoulders relaxed like a slack puppet before being pulled upright again.

Ashlyn felt the air shift, colder than it had been before. There was a second thread humming beneath the first. This wasn't just Onita. Someone else was here.

Marcus's gaze bolted ahead, not at Naomi but beyond her. When he spoke, it was just as emotionless as Naomi.

"He betrayed us," he said. "Meant to turn over our posts to the British. Said you were leverage. You were a bargaining chip."

He stopped, swallowed.

"I found the letter with his stuff. Stuffed in a map case, buried behind old scout notes. It was encoded, but I knew the cipher. Names. Dates. Movement on the river. Where the Seneca camp was. Where the French wagons would sit."

He blinked. "I turned it in. Took it to the command tent myself. They told me I had forged it. That it was a lie. Maybe British misinformation. They told me to forget it."

Ashlyn stepped forward. "What did they do with the letter?"

"They kept it. They told me it would go into the intelligence file, but it never went."

Now, his gaze was somewhere far away, tone out there as well. "Weeks later, it was gone from the command file. Tucked somewhere it didn't belong, buried in a supply ledger or a shipping manifest. Out of sight."

Naomi's eyes clouded. The surrounding energy began to fade and loosen its grip on her, but her voice dripped bitter sorrow.

"You might be right," she said in a whisper. "But it was never your place."

Now Marcus blinked again, brow wrinkled. "Wait, what?"

Naomi breathed out and fell back into Ashlyn's arms, unconscious once again. Onita had vanished.

Marcus took a halting step back as if waking from a dream. He looked at Ashlyn, eyes wide and bewildered.

"What just happened? What did I say?"

Ashlyn could only stare at him. "You don't remember?"

Branches snapped above them, and a moment later voices permeated the trees.

"There they are!" someone yelled. It was the paramedics.

Flashlights flickered through the thick brush as two EMTs battled their way through the woods, with Marcus waving them in with quick arm motions.

"Down here," he yelled. "Be careful; it's steep."

Ashlyn scooted aside as the paramedics climbed down the hill, doing their best to keep their footing. Zac hovered close to Naomi, still pale and flicking his eyes between Naomi and Marcus.

The lead EMT knelt beside Naomi and began checking everything while the others found a place to put the portable stretcher and medical bag.

"She fell from the bluff," Megan said in a calm voice. "Head injury. Came to for a few moments and then she fainted again."

Ashlyn added softly, "She just seemed disoriented and then faded out..."

No need to complicate things for them.

The paramedic was already working. "Pulse is strong. Breathing is steady."

He moved with efficient care, checking for any spinal injury, securing her neck, lifting her onto the stretcher like there was nothing to it. The group stepped back to let them work. Ashlyn glanced at the tree where the piece of fabric was still flapping in the wind and then at Marcus, who was still standing stiffly, quietly staring into space.

"You really don't remember anything of what you said?" She asked, voice low.

Marcus shook his head, jaw clenched. "I remember the look on her face. And then... nothing. Like I blinked and lost ten minutes."

He paused. "But something's... off. Like it's still in the back of my head. Like a dream I almost had."

The paramedics started back up the bluff, carrying Naomi, with Megan and Zac right behind them, shining their flashlights on the uneven trail.

As they made their way back toward the fort, Ashlyn tapped Zac's arm and said just loud enough for only him to hear, "We'll regroup tomorrow, do more research, and maybe one last investigation."

Zac nodded, but the enthusiasm he normally had was gone. He tapped his fingers on his thigh and looked everywhere but at her.

"Yeah," he mumbled. "Whatever you need."

Megan fell back to walk with Ashlyn, slowing her pace while she did so. "Am I going to need to pull the plug on Living History?"

"Not yet. I've got until tomorrow, right?"

"Yeah. You have one more day."

They walked for a few more moments. The clearing came back into view, and the grove where it had all started, and where so much had ended. Ashlyn stopped at the foot of the old tree, placing her palm on its bark. The tree that had held so many secrets now contained only silence.

"I heard you," she whispered.

Something shifted in the shadows, softer than movement, but real. Then she turned and followed the other three.

CHAPTER NINE

Chapter 9

Ashlyn stirred just before dawn. Soft gray was creeping across the edges of the sky, and the early birds had begun their tentative songs. She remained still, listening, and finally let out a breath. She was amazed to be awake at all since she had crashed into bed bone-tired and threadbare just hours before.

Something had shifted, and she understood what she was supposed to find. What still astounded her, even after years of this work, was that there were spirits (and people) and so many still trapped in their stories. Hundreds of years, and some griefs were louder than any cannon. There would not be a straightforward answer to this one. No ceremony to clear it away. Only truth.

It was a good humility check that perception is every-thing. Everybody sees the world through their own lens of hurt. That was what made people, and ghosts, so messy. Emotions never stayed in the nice, neat boxes you tried to contain them. Relationships were even worse.

Naomi had been released from the hospital late the night before, bruised, but okay. Ashlyn had gotten the message around two, a brief text from Megan: *She's safe. Sleeping. I'll keep her close.* It helped Ashlyn fall asleep, but it hadn't erased the tension in her chest.

Her phone buzzed. She did not flinch, but she startled how well it aligned with the direction of her thoughts, as if they had summoned him.

The screen showed 5:34, and a text from Rhys: *Call when you wake up.*

She stared at it. Part of her wanted to. Yearned for his steady voice, and the grounded presence he always had. Another part, the part that was still raw from the emotion-al unraveling of last night, froze.

She didn't want to talk to him yet. Not after how vul-nerable she'd felt. Not that Rhys would judge her; that wasn't the issue; she was the issue.

How do you open the door to intimacy without know-ing what part of yourself will walk in? Ashlyn pulled the blanket a little tighter over her shoulders, pressing the phone against her chest. She hadn't intended to let him in, but grief had a way of peeling everything back. Now, on this pale blue morning, she did not know what version of herself he'd seen or what version she was willing to be.

All she could do was roll the dice. Ashlyn tapped the FaceTime icon, and it rang only once before he appeared, bathed in soft morning light and framed by the familiar comforts of a messy bookshelf in the background. Rhys looked like himself: sharp-eyed and beautiful in that soft, unassuming way he had. There was always something steady in his eyes.

"Hey," she said, her voice still a little raw from sleeping.

"Morning," he replied. "You look... like someone going through it."

She smiled, pulling her hair back with her fingers. "You're not wrong."

"Did I wake you with my text?"

"No, you're fine. I was awake." She paused. "Just... one of those nights."

He leaned into the screen as if studying her face. "The case?"

"Yeah," she paused. "It's messier than I expected. There is grief, but there is also so much love, resentment and guilt. I don't even know whose story it is anymore."

Rhys lifted his brow. "That's usually when it's worth telling."

Ashlyn looked down. "It's more than. The haunting is... personal. So much emotion tied to just that place. It's not just noise; it's not just the stage but a reenactment of the original."

"And you're just stuck in the middle."

She didn't answer, just looked at the screen. The concern in his eyes was real; there was nothing contrived about it; there never was. That was what made it so difficult.

"I thought I understood it. But it keeps getting further away from me."

"Maybe it just wants to be understood? It doesn't want a resolution."

The ache in her chest expanded slightly. She hadn't realized how badly she needed to hear something so simple.

"I don't know," she said. "Sometimes I feel like I'm just the lens, not the camera. Like I'm not really a part of anything, just... letting it all pass."

"And that's how you know it's real. Spirits don't use mirrors. They use people."

Ashlyn chuckled lightly. "That's disturbingly poetic."

"I'll put it on a bloody card," he said, deadpan. Then softly: "You know, you don't have to carry it alone."

That one sentence was way too close to something she hadn't allowed herself to name.

"I should get back to it. Prep starts soon."

Rhys studied her closely. He didn't argue; he just changed his tone, as if he were moving carefully around something he valued. "Alright. Just... don't vanish. At least let someone know where you're going."

"I won't." She paused. "Thanks Rhys. For being... you."

"Always," he said. No uncertainty.

After hanging up the phone, Ashlyn sat with herself for a long time. She felt like she could trust him, but part of her still flinched at trusting anyone. What if she was wrong about him too? What if the ghosts were not the only ones playing out old patterns? There was no good in ruminating about something impossible to resolve right now. Time to get to work. Zac had said he would be in early, and she needed to shower and gather her thoughts before meeting him. Just after 7 a.m., Ashlyn found him outside the archive building, sipping two cups of coffee.

"You're the best," she grinned, taking one. "How did you sleep?"

"I didn't," Zac admitted, giving a sleepy grin. "Too much swirling in my brain."

"Yeah. I totally get that."

They walked inside, and the air was still cool and dry. The fans buzzed as they settled at the long center table.

"What are we hunting today, boss?" Zac said with a little too much forced enthusiasm.

Something was bothering him, had been since last night, but she let it go for now.

"We are going to find proof Henri was a traitor," she finally said, opening up her notebook. "At least something Jean-Claude may have interpreted as treason. Possibly a supply list or shipping manifests. Something with names, and movements or communicated interceptions."

"Got it," Zac said. "Some of the outdated French military documentation still exists on microfiche."

He directed her towards the machine in the back of the room, and together they grabbed a couple of reels from a labeled drawer.

"We're trying to get a grant to digitize the full collection," he added, sliding one of the reels in the reader. "But nothing has come through yet."

Ashlyn made herself comfortable alongside him, sipping on her coffee while he adjusted the lens and started the crank. The screen flickered to white noise as the image of pages was magnified. Zac started going through the first reel, turning blurry columns of French cursive and degrading inventories.

"Here. This reel is from 1757 to the end of 1759," he said. "It is right in the window."

They continued working in comfortable silence. Zac handed her a stack of notepad sheets where he had scrawled a handful of notations to check later. Ashlyn cross-referenced them against dates she recorded from the quartermaster's journal.

Then, something caught her eye.

"Wait, can you scroll back a little?"

Zac turned the dial back until the image she was pointing at came into focus.

"Look at this entry," she said. "June 1, 1757. A shipment was recorded for storage, but..."

She leaned closer, frowning. "There is no signature from Henri. And the quartermaster never checked in the materials."

Zac whistled. "That is... suspicious."

Ashlyn continued to look down at the column. "And look here, Jean-Claude's note two days later about missing powder, and uniforms. But no Henri. Not directly."

"So it passed through him, but disappeared."

"Or was circumvented," Ashlyn said. "If Henri was passing supplies or information to the British, then that might be the hole that Jean-Claude found. Enough to trigger a confrontation. Can we print this?"

Zac shook his head. "Not from this machine. But I can transcribe it. Or you can take a photo."

She did just that, aligning her camera to the screen and capturing the fragile entry, with the faded ink dimmed enough to be reconstructed. Then she placed her phone down, eyes bright with renewed intensity.

"This is what Jean-Claude saw," she said. "It won't convict anyone of treason, but it is proof that something is awry when Henri was called into question."

Zac leaned back in his chair gazing at the screen, still lit. "So maybe Jean-Claude wasn't paranoid. Maybe he was correct after all."

Ashlyn didn't answer immediately. She stared at the flickering projection and then said, "Or he was paranoid and reading into nothing. At any rate, he felt that something was wrong."

The room became quiet except for the gentle whir of the machine, and just like that, the past felt a little closer. They shifted from microfiche and into the quartermaster ledgers, working through yellow pages material and brittle pages filled with cramped French handwriting. Ashlyn flipped while Zac scanned, eyes darting over each list of rations, troop sizes, and attributions.

Then she stopped and angled the book toward the light and saw something wedged in between brittle pages labelled Supply Trade, Early August. It was a slip of paper. She pulled it free and unfolded it.

"What is it?" Zac asked, leaning over her shoulder.

Her eyes moved across the rows of tight cursive. Some of it was encoded. Dates, names, regiment attributions, quantities for provisions, transportation routes, troop movements.

"This is it," she said. "This is what Jean-Claude was trying to stop."

Zac leaned in and read over her arm. "It's a communications log. And half is encoded."

"Which means Henri was doing more than just losing supplies; he was supplying information."

She was up, clutching the paper with a grip. "This proves it wasn't just a ghost story; it really happened. Jean-Claude wasn't just motivated by jealousy; he was trying to protect someone. Maybe everyone."

She exhaled a large breath, already thinking ahead. "We need to bring this to the grove tonight. If they have been stuck this long, it is only because no one knew the whole story."

"Yeah. That makes sense."

Then she looked back up, half-expecting to see Zac mimicking her relief. He was not. He was standing a few feet away, arms crossed, gaze fixed somewhere on the floor as though it might open up and swallow him.

"You don't look that excited," she said.

He blinked and then squeezed out a small smile. "No, I am. It's just," he rubbed the back of his neck. "It's a lot."

Ashlyn cocked her head. "Zac?"

He flinched at her voice.

"You don't look like you just solved a 250-year-old mystery."

He let out a thin breath, tried to smile, and couldn't. "I think I thought it would feel different."

Ashlyn waited. After a long moment, he sat down in the nearest chair, elbows on his knees. His voice was low.

"I didn't just find the haunting, Ashlyn. I... nudged it."

Her chest went cold. "What do you mean?"

Zac looked up, and for a moment, the mask he wore dropped.

"The faulty equipment, the flashlight at three a.m.? That was me. I rigged the timer. And the scratches... I did those myself. Just enough to make it plausible."

Ashlyn didn't say anything. Zac continued after a moment, his voice raw now, as if he needed to get it out.

"I never meant for anyone to get hurt. I swear. I just—Naomi was pulling away. Ever since last year, since Marcus... I figured if she thought something was happening she'd let me participate. She believes in this stuff, this history, this location. I thought maybe if I got absorbed in that…"

He trailed off with glassy eyes.

Ashlyn crossed her arms. "You faked a haunting."

"I figured if I made it up just enough to get her to believe, she'd turn to me and I'd protect her. I never expected Megan would want to be involved. And I certainly didn't expect her to hire you."

Ashlyn swallowed the lump forming in the back of her throat. Her voice was quieter when she asked, "Was it you? In the ski mask?"

Zac's breath caught. He looked away for a second, then nodded slowly. "Yeah," he admitted. "It was me."

Ashlyn stared at him, stunned. "You grabbed her."

"I wasn't going to hurt her," he said quickly. "I just wanted to scare her. Just a little. I was going to run away, make it look like something strange was happening. And then I'd be the one she turned to."

He raked a hand through his hair. "But Marcus was there. He ruined everything."

Ashlyn stared at him for a long moment.

"You weren't protecting her," she said. "You wanted to be chosen."

Zac winced but said nothing.

She exhaled heavily through her nose and pressed her palms flat on the table between them; her knuckles going white.

"There really is something here," she snapped. "Actual manifestations. History. And you…" She held herself in check, clenching her jaw, then pressed on. "You threaded your little performance right through it."

Stepping back, she paced once. "Do you have any idea what that does to someone like me? To my work? My name?"

Zac said nothing. His silence was fuel to the fire rising behind her ribs.

"You were there last night," she continued, low but furious. "You felt that energy. At the well. In the grove. You saw what we saw, and you still chose to lie about it."

She spun back at him now, eyes narrowed.

"You don't get to do this because you have an irrational fear of not being seen or heard. You don't get to manufacture fear and pretend that it was being caring."

"I know." Zac groaned, shame flooding across his features.

Ashlyn let that hang for a moment, then her voice cooled, but didn't lose its bite.

"You didn't have to be a ghost to be seen, Zac. You had to show up. As yourself. I mean, I guess that just wasn't dramatic enough."

Zac flinched again.

"I'll tell Megan," he said. "What I did. I'll take ownership."

Ashlyn once nodded, but her jaw was still tight, and that wasn't enough.

"No. You don't get to 'take ownership' in a side conversation with Megan. You tell Naomi."

His eyes were wide. "Ash-"

"She was the reason you even did this in the first place, wasn't she?" Ashlyn snapped. "You were trying to stage a haunting so that she would need you. You tried to bring her into a dangerous situation, and now you owe her the truth."

Zac swallowed hard. "I never wanted her to get hurt. I swear."

"Don't you see, Zac? You lied to her." Ashlyn said. "Lied to all of us. You bent her trust by using fear getting close to someone who already has too many reasons to live in fear and not trust."

He couldn't look her in the eye.

"Zac." Ashlyn leaned in closer to him. Lowering her voice, but just as sharp. "You don't get to say you care and then play God with people's perceptions. Do you know what that could have done to my reputation? What if I hadn't caught it and something went south, someone was hurt. I mean, hell."

"I will tell her everything."

Ashlyn stepped back, arms folded across her chest. Her pulse still buzzed under her skin.

"Good. Because no one deserves the truth more than she does."

Something still didn't sit right with her.

"That night in the grove. You said you saw Naomi and Marcus both. Before they disappeared."

Zac's brow furrowed. "Yeah. I did."

"You're sure?"

He looked up. "Yes. I saw Naomi heading into the trees fast, like she was being followed. Marcus was right behind her. I went after them."

"But Marcus was never there."

"I know," Zac said, shaking his head. "I know. That's what doesn't make sense. I followed them into the woods. But when I got to the clearing, there was no one. Just me until you found me."

"You really saw them?"

"Yes."

"I don't think you saw Marcus. You saw Jean-Claude."

Zac blinked. "What?"

Ashlyn's mind raced, threads snapping together. "You saw a man chasing a woman into the woods. You believed it was Marcus, because that's who you expected to see near Naomi, but this spirit, we've already seen it mimic behavior. Reenact patterns. Jean-Claude reliving the past... That's what you walked into. Residual trauma playing out like a loop."

Zac looked pale now. "But it felt real."

"Because it was. Just not the way you think."

"Go apologize to Naomi and Megan," she said. "Then we all meet at the grove tonight. We've got one more story to set right."

Zac nodded, quiet and pale, the truth hanging heavy. Ashlyn said nothing more; there would be time for consequences later.

The next few hours passed quickly. She had invited Megan, Zac, Naomi and even Marcus to the Grove at ten that evening. She had also told Megan that Living History Week was a go, and she would understand why soon enough.

She spent the rest of the day preparing herself mentally, physically and spiritually. She packed the letter, the page from the ledger, her crystal, and a small drawstring pouch filled with salt and cedar shavings. Nothing flashy. Just anchors.

Then she changed into dark jeans, boots, and a t-shirt, then paused in front of the mirror to see who was going to walk into the woods tonight. Ashlyn Alden. Psychic investigator. Truth-teller. Witness. Let the ghosts come.

The grove was quiet when Ashlyn arrived, the last traces of daylight clinging to the tops of the trees. She walked the perimeter first, then crossed to the center, where the old tree stood like a sentinel. She knelt and placed her pouch of cedar, thread, and salt near the base of the trunk. Her recorder, a small digital one, was clicked on. She set it near the roots, then sat back on her heels and waited.

Megan and Naomi arrived together. Ashlyn stood as they entered the clearing. Naomi didn't look at her, but she gave the smallest acknowledgement. That was enough. Zac followed moments later, hands in his pockets. He kept his distance. The way Megan and Naomi held themselves made it clear: he'd told them.

Then Marcus appeared. He looked tired and drawn around the edges. It was clear the encounter had unnerved him, but there was a steadiness to him tonight. They formed a loose ring around the tree, and Ashlyn lit the candle, its stubby wick flickering to life. She laid the folded letter beside it, weighed with a stone.

"We brought the truth," she said. "That's all we ever owed you."

The wind stirred, and the leaves rustled.

"This letter," she continued, "contains dates, names, routes. It's encoded, but it's real. Jean-Claude saw it. And it changed everything. He believed Henri was a traitor. Maybe he was right. Maybe he wasn't, but he acted on what he believed to be true."

She let the silence linger.

"To Onita," she said. "You bore the weight of both men's choices. I don't know if you ever truly got to speak for yourself."

The recorder hissed, the sound of static rising, then cleared again.

Ashlyn glanced at it but didn't stop.

"We're not here to rewrite your story. Only to witness it. To honor what was lost."

The candle guttered once, then steadied. Somewhere near the edge of the clearing, the air shimmered in the way it always felt before something crossed.

Ashlyn didn't look for shapes. She didn't need to. She could feel the grief and rage. The sorrow caught at the roots of the old tree. After a long moment, she reached out and clicked off the recorder. Just then, the wind passed through the grove again, softer this time. Like a breath let go. It was done.

Then Naomi turned to Zac. "Walk with me?"

They stepped away together, moving through the underbrush, voices low and indistinct. Marcus lingered a moment longer, gave a small, tired smile, and then walked out on his own.

Megan came to stand beside her.

"Thank you," she said. Her voice was quiet. "I don't even know what else to say. You helped give them peace. And... us too."

Ashlyn's gaze was still on the tree.

"I won't press charges," Megan added. "Zac's got a lot to work through, but he was honest. Eventually. That counts for something."

"It does," Ashlyn said. Her voice was quieter now, less raw, but still steady. She hesitated, watching the flame dance in the stillness.

"I have an idea."

Megan glanced over, brows lifting. "For what?"

Ashlyn didn't answer right away. She looked through the bare branches arching overhead, into the night sky and then back down to the soft flicker of the candle at the base of the tree.

"For how we give them voice," she said. "And how we make sure we don't stop listening."

Chapter 10

The flames reached high, with a strange sort of aware-ness fire sometimes has. Shadows rippled on the battlements, and the crowd became quiet.

Standing just inside the boundary of the torchlight, Ashlyn Alden wore her dark hair down over her shoulders, a single thread of quartz dazzling at her collarbone.

"Stories linger in a place like this," she said, steady and low. "And Old Fort Niagara has more than its share. Some you know. Others, not yet."

The fire popped, as if in affirmation, and the breeze drifted in from off the lake. Ashlyn paused for a moment.

"You've probably heard tales of a headless ghost, the French soldier that still walks the ramparts, but ghosts don't just haunt. They remember, and sometimes... they wait for someone to get the story right."

Stepping back into the shadows, Ashlyn let flames illuminate the stage. Behind her, three figures stood half-shrouded in darkness.

The idea had come to her the day Naomi went missing, half-formed and already urgent. By the end of the night, she pitched it to Megan, who blinked once, said, "God, yes," and immediately began changing the schedule of events.

When she proposed it to Naomi, Zac, and Marcus, they were on board immediately.

Naomi had leaned into it first. "We tell it in three voices. One story, three truths."

Zac followed. "Let's use the battlements. Make it like a reckoning. Lanterns, or maybe torches."

Marcus, for all his edges, just nodded and said, "I'll write out Jean-Claude's side tonight."

They spent a long evening in the archive room writing the script, with their voices raised and lowered, adding nuance, shaping tone. Two hours after the event went live, it was sold out.

Now, the crowd occupied every bench and patch of stone, hushed beneath the low-hanging moon.

Back in the present, Ashlyn tilted her head back, towards the night sky.

"Three voices will speak tonight," she said, turning her body towards the crowd. "Each lived an iteration of what occurred here. Each wants a chance to be heard."

She stepped away.

"And maybe once the truth is spoken... they won't need to haunt us any longer."

The crowd felt silent, and in the distance an owl called.

Then Naomi stepped forward as Onita, taking her place in the torchlight. She was dressed fully in period Seneca clothing: a wrap skirt of deep hues, deerskin moccasins, and a beaded belt at her waist. Her dark hair hung in a single braid over her right shoulder.

When it came, her voice was clear.

"I was young in a time of war and change."

The fire crackled. Shadows danced on the stone.

"Our people, had lived on this land long before these walls were raised. Before the British or the French, but war came anyway. Not our war, but it reached us all the same."

She took a step forward, the beadwork at her collar catching the flame.

"The French courted alliances with the Haudenosaunee, though not always with honesty. Still, many among the Seneca sided with them, not out of loyalty to a flag, but as a shield against British expansion. The French treated us with more respect... at least, that is what we believed."

"We were not silent observers. Our leaders negotiated, advised, and resisted when they needed to. And women—"

She paused, looking out toward the audience.

"—held power in our ways. We chose our leaders. We kept our homes and decided on the future as best we could. I was not powerless. But I was not free of illusion either."

The torches burned brighter for a moment.

"I was invited to gatherings inside the French castle. They called them dances. Polite music, candlelight, soldiers in coats with brass buttons. I danced the night away while others planned battles outside the walls. Sometimes I wonder if it was wrong to enjoy those nights. To laugh when the world was burning."

"I met Henri there. He was a young officer, thoughtful, always watching the world around him. His French was careful. He listened and made me feel seen."

"Jean-Claude was different. Confident and charming in the way storms are. He was loud, unpredictable, impossible to ignore. I enjoyed his company, too. For a time, there was peace between them."

Her voice softened. The crowd leaned in.

"But peace is not meant to last when men believe they are owed something."

"One night, I was speaking with a friend beneath the walkway. I saw Jean-Claude walk toward Henri, his face tight with something I hadn't seen before. Henri followed. I didn't know it then... but it would be the last time."

A gust of wind curled around the battlements.

"I saw it happen. It wasn't a battle, not even a fight. Just a moment, a blade, and the consequence that followed. There was no honor in it. Jean-Claude made sure of that."

"I followed him. Watched him wrap the head in a cloth and bury it beneath the old tree. I said nothing that night."

She took a step closer to the front of the stage. Her shadow loomed tall behind her.

"I didn't act for vengeance alone. I acted to restore what was stolen, not just a life, but the truth of it. That's where honor lies."

"With my brothers beside me, warriors of our clan, I lured Jean-Claude to the clearing. The same clearing where Henri lay. There, I gave him no chance to speak. Not as a lover or a murderer. Only as a man who had taken too much."

She bowed her head, but not ashamed.

"That night, I did not weep. Not for Henri or Jean-Claude. I wept later, for what war does to love, and what power does to those who think they own others."

Then she raised her eyes.

"My voice was quiet. My name was louder in their mouths than it ever was in my own."

"Tonight, I say it for myself. I am Onita."

She turned, fading into the torchlight's edge.

Marcus stepped forward next, as Jean-Claude. His coat was French military blue, shoulders squared. He wore the role like a confession he hadn't realized was waiting inside him.

"He was my friend."

A pause.

"Henri was my brother in arms. We trained together. Bled beside each other in skirmishes that never made it into the journals. And I trusted him... until I couldn't."

"I saw the signs. There were maps missing, coded messages hidden in plain sight, French patrols ambushed just after he returned from scouting runs. I brought what I found to command. Documents. Inconsistencies. I thought they would act."

"But they dismissed it. Said I was seeing shadows. That I was... jealous."

The bitterness in his voice scraped the edge of civility. Marcus held it there.

"It's true; I envied him. Not for rank, but for the way she looked at him."

He looked at Onita, then back to the audience.

"But that's not why I acted."

"I believed with every part of me he was betraying us. That if I let him go unchecked, people would die. I thought I was saving lives."

"So I followed him. Confronted him. He reached for his sword first."

The firelight flickered.

"I told myself it was justice. That no court could have done what needed doing."

"But the truth is... I didn't wait for a verdict."

"I acted without judgment. I believed what I wanted to believe. Sometimes, I still think I was right."

"But I'll never know for sure, because the moment I drew my blade, the question stopped mattering."

He pulled back slowly and dramatically, allowing the silence to rub against him.

Zac emerged last from the shadows, as Henri, the firelight playing against the edges of his uniform. He wore a French officer's coat, but it was weathered, missing its trim. The sash was gone, and his boots were caked with dust.

Around his neck, where a cravat might once have been, was a strip of woven cloth, frayed and stained with time. He didn't stand like a soldier. He stood as someone who hadn't been sure he was welcome.

His voice, when it came, was soft.

"There are truths that you do not write in ledgers or reports."

He paused, looking past the group toward the dark walls of the fort, as if listening to distant drums.

"I saw what was coming. The French were losing ground. The British would take the fort, not if, but when. And I thought... if someone spoke first, someone who still had breath and reason, that perhaps... it wouldn't end in slaughter."

"I wasn't trying to defect. I was trying to prevent the inevitable and trade something smaller, quieter, for something greater."

He exhaled, not quite a sigh.

"I met with a British envoy. I offered useful information, patrol routes, and weaknesses in the walls. Not to get anything in return. To trade for mercy. I asked if they would spare the Seneca villages nearby, and that they would leave our allies untouched."

"I spoke of Onita. Not so much as a name to call upon, but as a reason to reconsider. I told them that her people honored every treaty, every alliance. That if they marched through here, they would trample over something sacred."

His hands tightened at his sides. "I thought if I made it personal, they might actually listen."

"But I underestimated what they were after. And I overestimated what I meant."

"By the time I tried to fix it... it was too late. Jean-Claude had already found my papers."

He turned slightly toward Onita, an expression of longing and hesitance painted across his features.

"I never meant to put you in danger. I thought I was protecting you and thought I could keep it from ever coming to you at all."

A silence stretched between them.

"I never raised my blade... but I still betrayed someone I loved."

He stepped back slowly and without defense, and stood in the firelight, unmoving, unspeaking, just... still.

Ashlyn stepped forward again, and no one moved. She let the silence expand in the same way grief stretched beyond generations.

She looked toward the tree line, to that quiet separation where the present blurred toward the past, and the past blurred toward memory. For a long moment, she stood there without moving, her breath moving in rhythm with the dark, as if listening to something only she could hear.

Her gaze drifted back toward the people gathered before her. Their faces were fogged into suggestion rather than detail, but she could feel them observing with the quiet reverence that came with a fear of a truth just out of reach.

Behind her, the battlements stood silent, the stones older than any of them, bearing witness as they always had. Somewhere nearby, a breeze stirred the tall grass, but no one turned to look. When she finally spoke, it was with intention.

"Three voices," she said. "Three truths."

She let the pause linger longer, but it was because the words deserved space.

"And maybe the story we've inherited was never the whole one to begin with."

"If you've ever been silenced," she said quietly, "if you've ever lost something to a story that wasn't yours..."

She let the silence hold again.

"...leave a stone."

There was a shallow wooden bowl outside the circle of the light to her left, and it was filled with smooth river stones. Ashlyn had chosen them earlier with a desire for something honest and real.

"It doesn't have to be loud to be remembered."

She tipped her head toward the old well, where stone met shadow and the past was almost close enough to touch. A few people cleared out and walked off that way, each of them quietly selecting a stone and placing it near the well like a memory being returned to the earth.

Ashlyn turned a little then. She had a feeling that drew her to the tree line just beyond the fort's edge. In that brief, suspended moment, she thought she saw them standing there.

Henri, Jean-Claude, and Onita.

They stood shoulder to shoulder at the edge of the woods, as if the space between now and then had been thinned just enough to let them through. No parades, no spoken words or gestures, only that something had fit into place, that by saying their names aloud, honoring their truths, had somehow circled them back into the same moment, united as they had never quite been in life.

Then, as naturally as it had come, the vision dissipated, and the three figures faded from substance to shadow, leaving only the sense that they had been.

Ashlyn remained until the last stone had been placed. Above her, the stars pressed closely, as if they too were listening. She did not have to speak. The fort had heard enough for an evening. Truth might not erase the past, but it had a way of setting it in its place. It wasn't closure, but it was a story spoken to its end.

This, she thought, is where honor lies.

About the Author

If you enjoyed *Where Honor Lies*, you might also enjoy other stories in the **Kindred Spirits Mysteries** series—standalone paranormal mysteries featuring psychic medium Ashlyn Alden and other unforgettable characters. Each book explores a haunting rooted in history.

Find all titles at: www.bethconnor.com

Join the Newsletter

Want behind-the-scenes extras, sneak peeks, and free stories?

Sign up for Beth Connor's newsletter and get a bonus scene from *Where Honor Lies*, plus early access to upcoming releases, exclusive content, and more.

Sign up on my website:
www.bethconnor.com

Leave a Review

Did this story stay with you?

Leaving a review on Amazon or Goodreads helps new readers discover the series. Even a short note makes a big difference and is always appreciated.Thank you for supporting independent authors.

About the Author

Beth Connor writes at the wild intersections of fantasy, science fiction, and whatever refuses to fit in neat genre boxes. Her work spans from the thrill-charged mystery of Lake 40 to the magic-laced realms of the Isdralan Chronicles, to the ghostly charm of her Kindred Spirits Mysteries.

Beth is a rebel storyteller at heart—a dancer turned choreographer turned teacher, a writer who sometimes argues with her own characters, and a former tech support agent who still thinks rebooting might fix the world. She's a mom, a dog mom, and a firm believer that adulting is mostly a myth. She's also married to a wonderfully patient man who somehow keeps up with the chaos.

She vibes with stoic philosophy, fears heights but not endings, and occasionally picks fights with genre labels. Her fiction leans hopeful, her characters rarely follow the rules, and her readers tend to be the kind of people who dog-ear pages and stay up too late. She also publishes anthologies, tap dances well enough to impress toddlers and grumpy cats, and believes stories don't always have to mean something—sometimes they just need to take you somewhere fun.

Find her anywhere people love books that blur lines, bend genres, and let imagination off the leash.

www.ingramcontent.com/pod-product-compliance
Lightning Source LLC
Chambersburg PA
CBHW010643190726

48289CB00009B/2834